Strobe Lighting
and other stories

Sian Hughes

Biscuit Press

Published 2013 in Great Britain

Biscuit Press
Washington
NE37 2HS

ISBN 978 1 903914 53 3

Typeset by Free Spirit Writers, Bridlington

Cover design by Colin Mulhern

With special thanks to my husband, and to family, friends and colleagues: Mike Hughes, Caroline Hughes, Matthew Bennett, Penny Hughes, Jerome Spaargaren, Sally Bennett; Ann Schlee, Kerry Beckett, Brigitta Ansdell-Evans, Blanche Sears, Robert Harrold, Ted Aves, Branwen Lucas; the Monday friends and the Morley friends and Penny Leube, Andy Peake, Sue Mellins, Ernst Leube, Fay Greene, Mike Walker and Brian Lister.

"Things as they are
Are changed upon the blue guitar."

Wallace Stevens
The Man with the Blue Guitar

"Each of these stories is a little novel in itself – or at least the novelist in me goes on with the story. This, to me, is a great compliment, for a short story is a masterly compression of something with implications that go on."

Diane Johnson

Contents

The Garden Party

Yesterday's weather arrived today which gave them both a shock. It arrived before dawn, when they thought they had got away with it and that the rain and high winds coming from Scandinavia – she thought it was Scandinavia when she glanced up at it from the crossword but then she had never really understood it since it had gone into different colours, in fact had never understood it at all, especially after the second gin and tonic – that the rain and high winds had passed them by altogether and wreaked their havoc on Shetland or the North Atlantic or somewhere more used to extreme climatic conditions. Henry had said they would be wrong. Remember that chap who wore nylon shirts and said no hurricane? They'd had to get a tree surgeon in after that. You could count on them being wrong. Guaranteed. And so they had left the garden furniture out overnight (it had been such a lovely evening) and now it lay strewn around the garden, white tubular frames overturned, striped orange cushions (how foolish not to bring them in) flung into the borders, against the delphiniums, against the standard roses, limp, flattened, their cheerful suburban buoyancy destroyed.

And Jasper was coming home. Jasper, her son, her son not Henry's, who at the time of the divorce had chosen to live with his father – chosen. How can you do that, at twelve, how can you make that choice? How can the courts allow it? The unnaturalness, the cruelty of it, still made her heart race (something tearing at her insides) and tears prick behind her eyes. It hadn't been Henry, he hadn't been the one, she could imagine a boy taking against Henry but she hadn't known Henry then. No, it had been Peter, sweet, soft, lovely Peter who would have loved him and treated him as his own and was prepared to, told the courts he was prepared to, because he loved her so much, and then had stopped loving her because Jasper had been taken away from her and he took the burden of it.

She hadn't hated her husband – her now ex-husband, Jasper's father, then. She hadn't thought about him much, really, just got bored with him as she imagined he had got bored with her and dallied, because she had the time, and after a while found Peter and was astonished by the vitriol, and the fight her soon-to-be ex-husband had put up, and won. So that the access days, the access weekends, were tinged with the hatred she had now for her son's father and in a strange way for her son as well, because he had not chosen her, and she loved him so much. And now he was coming home, Jasper coming home, with his new wife, and the garden looking such a mess.

She had bought the gazebo, bought it at the garden centre, because, well, what she'd had in mind was a garden party, a little garden party, where she would invite friends from the village, and perhaps a few of her particular women friends (and where are they going to stay? Henry asked) and it would be a warm, intimate but elegant summer party in the garden, their delightful garden which she sometimes opened up under the National Gardens Scheme, and everyone would have a happy time, and it would all seem so normal, Jasper coming home.

And how lovely it was going to look, the garden, seen from under the white canvas sails, the long table (not too long) laid so that Jasper and his new lovely wife would be looking out into it, but protected from the sun, the hot sun, or a sudden summer shower, with herself and Henry at either end. Just the four of them, when the other guests had departed. She had seen the tableau, it was already on her retina, the table settings, the cloth, the silver, the glass, the crisp white napkins and the napkin rings. Jasper's silver christening ring, beside his place. It had been found and already polished. It was going to be perfect, for Jasper.

Caterers would be hired, and a waitress. Henry, not really listening, had suggested Pixie, the teenage product of his first wife's second marriage. She lived in Brixton, not far for her to come. Do her good, a weekend in the country. But Amanda did not like the look of Pixie, or more accurately, she did not like the look of Pixie's lip piercings, preferring Rachel, a nice plump girl in the village. Were caterers strictly necessary? Possibly not, but she knew the vagaries of her own cooking, especially when flustered. Caterers were the safer option. And the menu would be stylish, on trend, everything that she was not.

A little like a wedding, she thought. The wedding she had not attended, not been invited to, in a vineyard in somewhere called Orange County. She hadn't known whether Jasper's father had been invited, was afraid to ask, opting to believe in 'just a few mates and Nic and myself.' Yes, it would be like a wedding and after all, she deserved a wedding, didn't she? As Jasper's mother.

He was too late to stop the gazebo, which arrived before he knew what it was for, and which he referred to alternately as the bivouac or the mosque, but Henry had put his foot down about the garden party. Once he focussed on it, he couldn't imagine what on earth she thought she was doing. It was stiff, formal, completely over-the-top. Who was going to enjoy it, did she imagine? Not Jasper, for starters. Not his wifelet, who was bound to be a bag of nerves anyway. She had got carried away, allowed herself to be carried away, hadn't thought it through. It was all a ridiculous amount of show and expense and he was not going to fund it. Get that clear. 'Sorry, old thing,' he said, putting his arm round her shoulders because he loved his second wife, or was fond of her at least, never having had much idea what loving meant, 'it's not really about the money. I'd do it if I thought it was anything like a good idea, but it's not. It's too much, too much for them and too much for you. You need the whole thing to be as natural and stress-free as possible, after everything that's gone on.' He kissed her. 'It'll probably be horrible weather, anyway. You know I'm right, really.'

And looking out over the early morning garden, she knew that he was. He came downstairs and out on to the wet grass to join her. He was wearing slippers and maroon striped pyjamas, as tragic and defeated as anything in the herbaceous border. 'Ghastly mess,' he said. 'But the bivouac standeth.'

'Only just.' The gazebo stood by the terrace, a sort of three-sided tent. Rain had pooled on the flimsy canvas roof and dripped steadily through the seams. What had seemed elegant and appropriate yesterday looked cheap and pretentious today. 'I wish you wouldn't call it that.'

'I'll get Jamie Wilson to come round and help me take it down.'

'Would you? It looks so awful now.'

'I'll go in and give him a ring. He can put it in the garage. What time do they arrive?'

'Eleven thirty-ish.'

'Right-ho.'

'Thank you, darling.'

'The champagne's on ice,' he said as he turned to go. 'If the weather picks up we can open the French windows.' He gave her a thumbs-up. Poor Henry. He was doing his best. It wasn't his fault that he could be deeply irritating.

She went upstairs to dress and wondered, for the millionth time, what she would be like, this wife that Jasper had chosen, chosen over all the girls he might have chosen. Nicky, Nicola. Australian. That was good. Friendly, open. Less judgemental, perhaps, of a mother who had not been chosen, all those years ago.

They had met, Jasper's letter had said, in the States. Jasper's father had sent him there, after his disappointing 'A' Levels. Jasper had not been bright. He had not worked, his father said, had fooled around, not appreciated the sacrifices made for such an education. (Though his housemaster had told him, had told them both, that this was not so. He did work, he just didn't achieve very much. There were boys like that. He was a nice boy). But his father had decided that he must learn some manual skill, learn to shift for himself, life is not a bowl of cherries, and had sent him out to his godfather, a timber merchant in Seattle. She was sad that he should have been sent away when all that was wrong with his work was that he was not very good at it. He had liked his school, his father's old school. She wondered whether her ex-husband's subsequent wives had not had a part to play in it all. She remembered the events – the Open Days, the Sports Days, with herself, Henry, Jasper's father and stepmothers one and two. It had never been easy. Some fractured families seem to manage it, all bright new smiles and hats, but not theirs. She had not seen Jasper since they had waved him off at Heathrow, one summer's evening, thirteen years ago.

Nicola was from Melbourne. She had a job with an advertising company and Jasper had known her for five years. She was bright, funny, gorgeous. She was his dream woman.

She hears the taxi. It is arriving uncertainly, as taxis do. Unlike delivery vans, screaming up the driveway. Unlike FedEx. She had wanted to meet them, would have met them at the airport willingly, she and Henry, but they had preferred to take a taxi.

She knows she must get this right. Get this right if she gets nothing else right in the rest of her life.

She sees Henry behind the taxi, helping the driver unload the luggage. He is setting the cases down by the front door, where he will wait, where she knows he will wait, for the welcome. Jasper, his back to her, is handing Nicola out of the cab.

She goes to her and puts her arms around her. 'Nicola, my dear, how really lovely to meet you. Thank you for coming, thankyou. And welcome.'

She kisses her, and takes her hands, and smiles into her face, registering the scene behind, her son paying off the driver, fumbling the change. He turns and comes towards her, arms outstretched, and, still holding her daughter-in-law by the hand, she steps forward to greet him.

And to the taxi driver, reversing slowly away from the house, they might almost have looked like a family.

Mr. Rankin of Albuquerque

The other waiting passenger is in his late fifties, elegant as only tall people are allowed to be. He wears a classic stone Burberry, toning cashmere scarf and brown trilby, and carries a worn hide briefcase bearing his initials. The care with which the ingredients of his outward persona have been assembled suggests Italian, or possibly American, the latter confirmed as he boards the bus and negotiates his fare. As he slips into his seat he removes his hat. Some men carry grey hair or male pattern baldness with distinction. His is a sort of re-birth, soft tufts of baby-grey hair sitting curiously on an ageing, infantile head. Travelling from London to Oxford at seven o'clock in the morning, she had taken him to be an academic, a visiting professor possibly, but this unexpected head opens up other possibilities.

She could have smoothed it, sitting behind him, and indeed the damp, wispy hair invites it, as does a baby's after a warm woollen bonnet has been removed. How women wrap and unwrap their infants, like little hot parcels. No wonder rage rises in those creased pink faces. The Duchess had known a thing or two.

Unexpectedly, he does it for her, standing up and flattening his hair with his hand as he turns to look down the bus. Observing the seat beside her to be unoccupied, he picks up his briefcase, slides his hat along the luggage rack (does it always have to sit above his head, even when not physically on it?), says 'Excuse me', and sits down beside her. On her gloves, in fact, which she has not quite had the time to remove. She can see the fingers pointing towards her. The thought of whipping them out, suddenly, from under him, delights her. She does not quite have the courage.

'You're sitting on my gloves.'

'I beg your pardon?'

Americans never catch you on the first throw. She had noticed this phenomenon when living in Boston. The times she had repeated a perfectly straightforward statement. She was a travelling TEFL course.

'My gloves. You're sitting on them.'

'I beg your pardon.' This time without the interrogative. He raises himself an inch, slides the gloves from under him and lays

14

them carefully on her knee as a waiter might lay a Dover sole on a plate, without touching her.

'Thank you.'

'You're welcome.'

He lifts his briefcase on to his lap and snaps open the brass clasps, revealing a carefully folded sheaf of manuscripts in galley-proof form. He takes from his breast pocket a pair of half-moon glasses and adjusts the beam above his seat. 'I needed to get a better light,' he says, inclining his head very slightly towards her, without meeting her eye. 'The bulb above my seat had blown.'

'Oh. I thought you moved to sit next to a fascinating woman.'

'No.'

Sense of humour failure. She doesn't feel embarrassed. It had been worth a try.

She takes up her Salman Rushdie - a bus journey is as good a place as any to make an inroad into a big book - and tries to immerse herself in what Malcolm Bradbury had once described as 'the beat and bounce of the writing, the glissando of presentation and performance.' But somehow it wasn't beating and bouncing for her and if there was glissando, it was of her thoughts. She would like to know about him, she would like to ... break him a little.

'What area of London is this?'

She looks quickly out of the window. Homebase flashes by on their left, a monument to failed aspirations. 'Acton.'

He checks his wristwatch and returns to his proofs. Heavily laced with graphs and tables, they do not look a fascinating read.

For a while Rushdie's exotic hero vies for supremacy with the quiet American, and in truth Zogoiby should have won, this Indian Portuguese Moorish Jew whose life passes at double speed. The trouble was, she didn't know anyone like that.

She feels him lean against her and sees that he has fallen asleep. His glasses are slipping slowly down his nose, their descent accelerated by every jolt and brake of the bus. She puts her hand out and catches them. Then she puts them on the top of her open handbag, to be returned when he awakes.

At Gloucester Green they both make for the taxi rank. Arriving a moment ahead of her, he takes the first taxi, pausing briefly on the open door to say: 'Excuse me. I have an appointment. Or I would offer you a lift.'

Miranda is waiting for her in the restaurant. Miranda is the nearest she has to a female relative. She is her late husband's daughter by his first wife, and lived with them during the early years of their marriage. Since it was death, not sex, which had deprived her of her mother, she had not resented her father's new wife, acknowledging that it was probably her presence that had turned his mind from sending her, at sixteen, to boarding school. She had finished her education at her London day school and she was grateful for it. Now she is in her third year at St. Hilda's, living with her boyfriend. Her father hadn't liked it but her stepmother has known when to hold off, and the two women share an easy, uncommitted intimacy.

'How was your journey?'

'Fine, thanks. I read most of the way.'

'Oh, what?'

'A Salman Rushdie. Not the latest.'

'Any good?'

'I don't know. When I say 'read' I mean 'had the book open.' I was distracted by a quiet American sitting next to me.'

'Oh?' Miranda raises her eyebrows knowingly.

She laughs. 'Not what you think. In fact he was quite irritating. And he had funny hair.'

'Toupé?'

'No. Transplant, I think,'

'Yuk.'

'I know. It turned him from an academic into a business executive at a stroke. MD of an international software company under pressure from below. Actually, I don't think he was either. He was correcting proofs, scientific or medical. He had an appointment in Oxford.'

'Blackwells, I should think.'

'Probably.'

When she comes to pay the bill she finds she still has his glasses in her handbag.

They leave the restaurant together and walk down St. Giles and into the Broad. It is raining and their umbrellas jar against each other in the crowded street.

'What are you going to do about the glasses?'

'Hand them in to the bus company.' He would have missed them, but only in the sense of realising that they were not there. He was the kind of man who would carry a second pair.

'You could drop them in at Blackwells. We have to pass it.'

They say goodbye outside the bookshop and she goes inside. A helpful assistant tells her that the medical and scientific editorial offices are now at Osney Mead but that she will telephone through to see if the American gentleman has indeed had an appointment. The train of enquiry now set in motion is already regretted.

The assistant sets down the receiver with an air of accomplishment. 'Yes. A Mr. Rankin. He just left. He's taking the next bus back to London.'

'Rankin?'

'Mr. Rankin of Albuquerque. You might catch him, if you're travelling back yourself.' The assistant, she can see, has Mills and Boon in her eyes.

She walks towards the bus station. It is raining heavily now. Rain in her eyes, traffic in her ears, traffic slowing down, heaving forward, forcing hidden tarns of gutter water on to shoes, tights, trousers. To a driver, city traffic is inert. To a pedestrian it is an impelled, articulated, mechanical beast capable of sudden and inexplicable attack. By the time she reaches Gloucester Green her legs and feet are soaking cold.

Bay number three. Through the steamy windows she sees that the bus is already filling up. She climbs in and walks down the aisle, stepping over wet rucksacks and anoraks. Every seat is taken. She turns and starts for the door, stopping for a man to remove his raincoat. He folds it neatly and stows it in the luggage rack above him, carefully, beside his hat. Mr. Rankin of Albuquerque does not hurry.

'Excuse me,' he says, as he leans in to his seat, allowing her to pass.

She stops. The Blackwells assistant would have it that their eyes met. 'I have your glasses,' she says.

'I'm sorry?'

'I have your spectacles.' She opens her bag and hands them to him.

'Thank you so much. May I ask ...?'

'They fell off your nose this morning. I picked them up.'

'I see. How kind. You've been most kind.'

'Not at all.'

'Are you travelling back to London?'

'I'd like to be. But I see the bus is full. I'll take the next one.'

17

'I'm sorry.' He looks vaguely round the bus.

I can't let you do that. You've been so kind. Why don't we both take the next bus. Why don't you let me buy you dinner. A sudden decision. A swift cab ride. A small restaurant. La rage que l'on a pour les choses impossibles.

'Will you take my seat?' He makes a small effort to raise himself.

'No, please. It's quite all right. I'll take the next one. It's only half an hour. You mustn't inconvenience yourself for me.'

'If you're quite sure. In other circumstances I'd have been glad to. But actually I have an appointment.'

He settles comfortably into his seat.

Entertaining Carlotta

She tumbles into the narrow hallway, flowers in one arm, designer luggage on the other. Breathless. Confident. Contained.

'Darling.' Pressing herself and the flowers into her hostess's embrace. 'This is so good of you. Yes, I declare it. You are a star. And looking good, too.' Taking a step back, appraising. 'Yes indeed, after all these years.' She smiles.

A slim, tidy figure in black suit and high-heeled shoes. Mid-forties. Significant jewellery in gold, rings and bracelets. Heavy, dark hair cut short at the nape, swinging forward, longer at the sides. Sharp, geometric. She sets down the Louis Vuitton bag, straightens the jacket, pulls in the stomach. 'Not bad, are we. We have, as they say, worn well. Is so often the hips that go, is it not. You have children?'

'One, a son. Peter. At university.'

'I have none. There are' – her reflection in the hall mirror smiles back at her – 'compensations. Is so good to see you Deborah. We must talk. I take a shower, and then we talk. Chew the fat, as they say.'

Carrying the case, Deborah leads her upstairs. She shows her into a room with a bed and a desk and walls covered with photographs of school teams. 'Peter's', she says. 'Alan is using the spare room as a study at present.'

'Perfect. I shall enjoy the photographs of the nice young men.'

'If there's anything you need, don't hesitate to ask. Come down when you're ready, and we'll have some tea.'

'No. Tea I do not take. I join you for a drink at, shall we say, six-thirty? I have calls that I must make.' She is walking Deborah out of the room, already talking into her mobile phone.

Six-thirty, and she descends. She has put on a red silk shirt. It matches her lips, her nails.

'Alan', she says, hand outstretched. She says his name in the French way, Alain. 'We have not met. But as you are husband of my old school friend, I am sure we will go along very fine.' She accepts a gin and tonic – 'when in Rome' – with a smile and a little shrug of the shoulders. 'But really gin and tonic I quite like. Such an English drink.'

'But you are English?' He raises his eyebrows.

'Oh me,' she answers easily. 'I am citizen of everywhere and nowhere. Is many years since I am living in England, since I am in school with your wife. In my work I am speaking Spanish. And sometimes French and German also. Really, sometimes I forget how to say in English. Is embarrassing. One feels quite foolish.'

'I think you do very well. How many of us can speak two languages, let alone four? Schoolboy French is about all I can manage, and that badly.'

'But probably you have not the need. For your work, I mean.'

'Quite. Chartered accountancy doesn't tend to attract linguists. Far too boring.'

'Not at all,' she touches his arm lightly. 'I am sure is most interesting. But is quite a different thing. For me, for my work, I must have languages.'

'And your work?' Alan takes her glass, refills it and returns it to her hand. 'Something to do with museums, Deborah tells me.'

'Exactly. I am museum curator. Actually,' she takes a sip from the glass and leans back, 'is the premier museo in Buenos Aires.'

'Which one is that?' Deborah has come into the room and sits down beside her.

'Yes. And for this I must travel. I have no choice. After London, here with you, I must to Paris. Possibly also Berlin. And then – hallelujah – home. Yes, I think I can say it, after so many years, Argentina is my home. But always I am happy to be in London and to see,' she raises her glass to Deborah's, 'old friends.'

'Charming woman.' Alan is undressing before the mirror. 'Good old St. Ursula's. Didn't know they turned out women like that.'

'Women like what?'

'Dunno. International. Citizens of the world. How friendly were you at school?'

'I can't remember.'

'What do you mean, you can't remember?'

'What I say. I can't remember. I can't remember her. She got in touch through the alumni website. '

'Why you?'

'Probably because we're conveniently located. She's trying to set up some exhibition or other in conjunction with the British Museum.'

'Did you check her out?'

'I tried to, but I couldn't find her.'

'Oh well. She's probably changed her name.'

'Debbie.' Carlotta is up early, has refused breakfast and is standing in the hall, putting on her suit jacket. A long silk scarf is wound round her neck, the back of her hair smoothed and checked.

'Deborah,' Deborah corrects her. 'You probably won't remember, but I always hated Debbie.'

'Of course. Deborah. How important these little things become as we age, do they not. Deborah. I give you my plan. One week I am with you – as I wrote in my e-mail. Each day I visit British Museum. I return at six, six-thirty and join you in your cocktail. I must buy your husband a bottle, indeed I must.' She reaches in her briefcase and takes out a little notebook and pencil. 'There. Gin,' she says, and snaps it shut. 'Of course some evenings I may have engagement. In which case I telephone you.'

'I should let you have a key. Just in case. I'll look one out and give it to you tonight.'

'So kind. So many thanks. I see you this evening.' She tucks her briefcase under her arm, turns to give Deborah a kiss on each cheek, and steps briskly out into the morning.

'We have this friend of Deborah's staying,' Deborah overhears her husband on the telephone. 'You must come over. Rather high-powered, a museum curator or something. In Argentina. Speaks three or four languages. And very good English.'

'She is English,' Deborah says, as he puts down the phone.

'Born English, perhaps. But really she's been in Argentina so long, Spanish is to all intents and purposes her first language.'

'We don't actually know how long she's been in Argentina.'

'It must be a long time. You can tell from the voice. I wonder what she did when she left school.'

'No idea.'

'Carlotta de Berg. Exotic-sounding name.'

'Very.'

In the evening Carlotta recalls the old days at St. Ursula's, reeling off a string of names of girls in her year, with whom she might have stayed, except that none lives quite conveniently for her present assignment. 'Jennifer Allison, Susan Barrie, Jean Templeman … you may remember them, Deborah, you may not. We were all, how shall I say, a little younger.'

'I remember those names,' Deborah says. 'The one I don't remember, Carlotta, is yours.'

'Of course not. I change it. And so would you. Charlotte Bergman. So heavy, so dull. You would not like that name, and nor did I. My friends, often they would call me Carlotta. You don't remember? A sort of diminutive. Affectionate. I liked it. And so I change. Is quite simple. But Deborah,' smiling over her glass, 'you must tell me about yourself. I long to know. My own life, you see, is very boring. Very, how you say, humdrum.'

'I shouldn't think so. All that travelling. All your languages. How long have you spoken English like – well, like you do.'

'Is different?'

'I think you must know it is.'

'How?'

'You speak it as if it wasn't your first language.'

'Is because I am so many years in South America. I marry, you see, very young. Seventeen. First girl from my year to be married. My husband, Jose-Maria, is Argentinian businessman and friend of my father. My father introduce us but I think he do not foresee such a result. Jose-Maria, he sweep me off my toes, I think you say. And for a while,' she looks wistfully at her listener, 'is very fine. We have apartment in Buenos Aires and I am learning Spanish. But then the father dies. Jose-Maria's father dies and Jose-Maria tells to me that we must move to the country, to the *estancia* of his father. Thousands of acres, thousands of cattle.'

'And you?'

'I go with him, of course. I am good wife. But I am young. And the *estancia* is full of women, the grandmother, the sisters, the servants, the mother-in-law. I do not like the mother-in-law. Like Spanish women, she cling too close to her son. Always we are arguing. And so I leave. I go back to the apartment in Buenos Aires. And after a while, Jose-Maria, he divorce me. Oh you must not feel sorry for him', she breaks off, laughing, 'already his mother has found for him a nice Argentinian wife, one who does not mind the grass and the cattle.'

'And you didn't marry again?'

'Oh yes. Two times more. But I have had enough of marriage. Is too complicated. Now I prefer lovers, young or old. Naturally

I prefer young. Oh, I am sure you think me very wicked,' she says gaily, 'but one must live one's life as one pleases. Is it not?'

Deborah finds Charlotte Bergman on the alumni website, but among the names of those with whom the school last lost touch. In the evening she brings the page up on her computer and shows it to Carlotta.

'Yes, I have seen this.' She leans forward, peering into the screen. 'Is quite wrong. I am in touch. I am very much in touch. I am here with you, in any case...' she breaks off. 'You should not concern yourself. Always these organisations are running on shoestrings. Always they get things wrong.'

A dinner party is arranged. Casual, a kitchen supper. Alan's friends are invited to meet the interesting guest, and she does not disappoint. Wearing a long black skirt and red satin blouse possibly a size too small, she charms with her fractured English and energetic re-telling of her life in Argentina, her husbands, her lovers, her work, her friends. Deborah, of course, is one of her oldest friends. Yes, they were at school together, but – how shall she put it? – not quite contemporaries.

'You ask how I become curator at the premier museo in Buenos Aires? I will tell you. My husband at the time – he was the number three husband and the last – yes, I can assure you, the last – my husband at the time, he was curator. I learn from him. And then he die. He have heart attack and die. And because I am there, and know how to do, I complete the exhibition he is working on at the time of his death. And they like what I do. And so it goes. And now, if my good friend Deborah will permit...' she jumps up from the table, offering to make the coffee.

'In the cafetière, yes?'

Deborah nods.

'Good. I make it how we drink in Argentina. Turkish-style. Very thick. Very strong.'

'Not too strong. At this time of night.'

'Oh, the English. Always so fearful. Always you think you will not sleep. Is not true. Is old wife's tale.' And she makes the coffee, thick and strong. She puts it on the tray which Deborah has laid, and carries it through to the sitting room.

'It's going well, your work?' The guests have left. Alan, fearing that he will indeed be kept awake, is making a pretence of finishing his coffee. Deborah is in the kitchen.

'Very well, thank you, Alain. Very well indeed. Very helpful people.' She leans back into the sofa cushions, pushes her shoes off with her toes. 'I rest my feet on sofa. If you think Deborah will not mind.'

'Of course not. Make yourself comfortable.'

'You are very kind. Is tiring. So much walking up and down so many corridors. Never is anything quite where you expect it.' She sighs. 'Also, is stressful. First major exhibition of primitive South American art, as I was telling to your friends. Is planned for next March. But I must catalogue it by end of year.'

'Quite an undertaking, I'm sure. Although I have to say I know nothing about South American art.'

'Why should you? I do not expect you to. I know nothing about your accounting. But Alain,' she slides her legs off the sofa and leans eagerly towards him. 'I tell you what I do. When my exhibition opens, I send you invitation. To special preview. Yes, you and Deborah. You must come. Make for yourselves a little holiday in South America and come to my exhibition. It is settled. I await you.'

'Alan. Carlotta. What do you think she's doing in London?'

'What she says she is.'

'I mean, do you think she really goes to the British Museum each day?'

'Of course. Why should you doubt it? Anyway you went with her yesterday.'

'That's just it. I didn't. That was the plan, but I didn't. When we got out at Russell Square she darted off. Made an apology and darted off. I never saw her again.'

'Running late, obviously. A lot on her plate. It's a very important exhibition. She told me.'

'But supposing she's a fraud? I mean, I couldn't find her on the website....'

'Why should she be? I think you're getting paranoid, if you don't mind my saying so.'

'What if she wants to come again?'

'What if she does? She's not doing us any harm. Look. She's a clever woman with an interesting job who went to your old school. What more do you want?'

24

Saturday is Carlotta's last day in London. She leaves on Sunday. She will spend the day at work and then she will take her friends to dinner. No, she insists. It is her treat, a thankyou for their hospitality. She waves aside objections, she has already booked a table. 'Claridges,' she says. 'Yes, I thought for my last night with my friends we could – how you say – slum it at Claridges.' She laughs. And here, she says, taking it from her handbag and handing it to Deborah, is the front door key, in case she forget. She has booked into a hotel near St. Pancras for her last night, as she takes the Eurostar to Paris early Sunday morning.

'So you see, already almost you see the back of me.' She smiles. 'We meet at seven-thirty. Early meal, for I have early start. I look forward.'

Carlotta is at the restaurant before them, has ordered and is drinking champagne. She is not alone. A dark-haired young man in open-neck shirt and designer stubble sits at the table.

'My friends,' Carlotta rises to greet them, arms outstretched. 'I thought champagne, no? to celebrate successful visit.' Her companion rises, offers his hand. 'Of course you do not know my researcher. His name is – yes – is Christophe.' She pats the chair beside her for him to resume his seat.

Waiters busy themselves around the table, taking coats, pushing in chairs, flicking away imaginary crumbs. Light bounces off the glasses, the silver-rimmed white plates.

'Deborah. Alain. How much I have enjoyed my little stay with you. And I hope, not too much trouble for you?'

'Of course not. Not at all.' Alan, expansive, is enjoying the Dom Perignon. 'A pleasure. You must come again.'

'You are very kind. I would not presume. Not even with so good friend as Deborah. I am sure, really, you are very glad to be, how you say, shot of me.' She laughs, a little self-deprecating laugh, her hand resting lightly on Alan's arm, staying his disclaimer. 'No. Is true. And really, a little meal is how I can do to thank you. And Alain,' lifting her eyes from the menu, 'if you will permit, I will myself order the wines. I should ask you to choose, for you must know much more than me, but' – and she wags a finger at him – 'I am sure you would be naughty and concern yourself about the cost, and this I cannot have, on my last night. No, with so fine food we must have fine wines. Is it not, my friends?'

Alan nods, rather feebly, in agreement. Christophe shrugs his shoulders. Deborah thinks she hears him say 'whatever' but Carlotta, talking over him, says 'he speak very little English.'

Carlotta puts on her glasses and studies the menu. Deborah, leaning back, relaxes into the pinks and peaches of her surroundings, the Art Deco opulence. The champagne begins to sing in her head.

Decisions are made. Carlotta applauds Deborah's choice of a starter of seared scallops and follows suit, instructing Christophe to do the same. Alan orders lobster and salmon ravioli. 'Good choice. I shall order a Muscadet to accompany, and if I have your approval, my friends, a red to follow. Yes?'

The red, a Chateau Margaux – Alan gulps as he hears the order – arrives with the main course and quickly disappears. Carlotta calls for another. When their puddings arrive a sweet white wine is poured, with port for Alan and Christophe, who have ordered cheese.

'Wonderful meal, Carlotta,' Deborah is savouring the Tokaji. 'What a treat.'

'My husband bring me here, many years ago. I am so glad you like.'

Alan leans towards her. 'So kind of you. So very kind.' He speaks slowly, conscious of the effects of alcohol.

Coffee is brought and Carlotta says something to Christophe. He stands up. Pushing back his chair, he places his table napkin beside the unfinished cheeses. She calls for a waiter to bring his coat.

'Yes, I am afraid he has to go.'

He kisses the hands of the ladies, bows briefly to Alan and, slinging his coat over his shoulder, saunters out into the street.

'He has much to do', Carlotta explains, 'before we leave tomorrow.'

Deborah is in the ladies' room. Alan, sipping his – he has just noticed – vintage port, watches the arrival of the bill. He sees Carlotta take it from the plate, unfold and smooth it out, check it, smile at the waiter. 'Is fine. Very good meal. Thank you.' She opens her slim evening handbag.

'No. This I do not believe.' She searches in her bag, looks up, searches again, takes out the contents and places them methodically on the table: lipstick, comb, compact, handkerchief, diary, mobile phone, keys, a tiny purse. She stares, rearranges them.

And then, still looking down, 'So stupid I have been. So stupid. You see how it is. I am stupid. I leave my cards in hotel safe. With my passport. Simply I forget to take them out. A woman on her own, travelling, you know… But this, really' – tears begin to gather behind her voice – 'I die of embarrassment.' She trails off, holding out her hands in a gesture of despair.

The waiter is beside the table with the handset. Alan draws it towards him, focuses on the bill, attempts to check it and, breathing deeply, takes out his card. Carlotta leans towards him. She takes the pen from the plate with the bill on it, notes the total, writes it down on a table napkin and folds it into her bag. 'I am so grateful, Alain. So very grateful. I send you cheque from hotel. As soon as I arrive. Immediate.'

Deborah is making her way back through the now crowded restaurant. 'Of course,' Alan says.

'Deborah.' They stand outside the restaurant, quiet in the calm of Mayfair. A taxi has been ordered for Carlotta. 'It has been such a pleasure to meet you again, after all these years. So much we have in common. In Paris I tell Janet Watson – you remember her? She is Janet Lefevre now – I tell her all about you. She will be so interested. Is always good to keep in contact, is it not. With old friends.' She kisses each of them on both cheeks and steps into the taxi, slamming the door shut as it moves away.

The crowded late night tube rattles back to Finsbury Park. They swing against each other, hanging on to the overhead bar.

'Fantastic meal, wasn't it?'

'Yeah.'

'I mean, you have to admit … And the wines. God. I hate to think what the bill came to.' She leans her cheek against her husband's arm. Light-headed, she giggles. 'As far as I'm concerned, she can come again – whoever she may be.'

'Yeah', Alan says, staring over her head at the passing tunnel.

The Inheritance

He looked again at the photograph, the wedding photograph. His father already frail, Christina in white. White, for heaven's sake.

'I'm contesting the Will,' he said. He'd wondered how it would sound, out loud, in the Knightsbridge restaurant.

'What?' She leaned forward, smiling.

'I said I'm contesting the Will.'

She settled back comfortably. 'That would be foolish.'

'Why?'

'It would be a waste of your money. The Will is watertight.'

Of course. It would be. Another tack, then.

'Half of what he owned. Two of the four houses, half his portfolio. You owe me that, surely. I am his son, for Christ's sake. His only son.'

'I am his wife. His widow. His next of kin.'

'I have children to educate – his grandchildren. He would have wanted it, knowing I'd lost my job.'

'He didn't know.'

'Because I didn't tell him. It would have worried him, with his heart and everything.'

His heart and everything. Even as he said it, he wondered if she'd known. Or if he'd hidden it from her, fearful of forfeiting this second chance at happiness with a younger, vigorous wife.

'It'll all come to you in the end, Edward.' Her voice was soft, fat, like her full figure, her face. 'Unless' – she raised the Pinot Grigio to her lips – 'unless, of course, I find myself to be with child.'

'Christ, you're a bitch, Christina. You're a prostitute. A middle-class fucking prostitute.'

'Winner takes all,' she said, and drained her glass.

Old Friends

How long had they been friends? It was hard to remember, they had all been alive such a long time. Charles and Celia, Angela and Elliot. The Caves and the Wilsons. Each couple somehow validated by the existence of the other. They came into people's minds together. Frequently, they came into people's lives together. 'Let's ask the Caves next Saturday evening.' 'And the Wilsons?' 'Why not? Good idea.' Probably they were expected to die together.

At seventy, Celia's life is a succession of little rituals. Her week has been lived almost before she has set foot in it. Monday, cleaning lady. Tuesday, Bridge. Wednesday, Italian class. Thursday, hairdresser. Friday, shopping. On Saturday she and Charles might take in a matinée (concessionary rate). And Sunday is lunch with the Wilsons.

She had often wondered, before his retirement, how Charles was to be accommodated into the mantra of her life. She need not have worried. Elliot had taken care of it, as Elliot had taken care of so many areas of Charles's existence.

They had known each other since university days. At Cambridge Charles had shone, taking a First in Classics and coxing the Cambridge boat in his two final years. Never to victory, Elliot was fond of reminding him. There had been that incident in 'forty-eight on the Middlesex bend when, looking back, he knew he could have taken the Oxford boat. A few seconds, a window of opportunity. It was not that he had not seen it. But the umpire's warnings, the fear of clashing blades, the ignominy of collision ... Elliot would have taken it. But Elliot was not a rowing man.

And then, the press cuttings. Charles had an unresolved, equivocal relationship with his press cuttings. He did not want them and he could not throw them away. They did not spare him. Keep them, his friends advised. To show the grandchildren. The advent of grandchildren might have forced a decision. But there were no children and no grandchildren and the torn, yellowing bundle remained to remind and to torment him.

After Law finals, Charles joined a partnership in the city. Elliot followed him a year or so later, an Upper Second in History converting to Law with a little more difficulty than he had anticipated. No-one at Case and Braeburn said, 'Charles has a first-class brain' more frequently, or more sincerely, than Elliot, yet when Millard Case finally stood down as senior partner it was Elliot, not Charles, who succeeded him. She remembered Charles, torn by his own disappointment and his loyalty to Elliot. He stood before her, his spare frame stooping slightly, his gaze not meeting hers. 'It's really a very good appointment. Elliot's the obvious choice. He's the wheeler-dealer of the practice, he brings in an enormous number of clients'. He ran thin fingers through his sandy hair.

'But you're so much better than him.'

'Better?'

'Brighter. Cleverer. You know. You always have been.'

'It takes more.' He looked at her puzzled eyes. 'All right, it takes something else. Something Elliot has, and I haven't.'

'Oh, Elliot, Elliot. Why didn't you join another practice? Why didn't he join another practice? Damn Elliot. Damn him, damn him, damn him. I bet he lied and cheated and ... wheeler-dealed his way into it.'

'He didn't.' He turned her shoulders, forcing her to meet his eyes. 'It isn't Elliot. It has nothing really to do with Elliot. I have to make you understand that. I can't change. Forgive me. I love you.'

For a long time he held her, stroking her fair hair, and then she had pulled away, drawing herself up against the long vistas of humiliation. But later she had sobbed into her pillow like a child, self-indulgently, for the lost hopes, for herself, for him, for her idea of him.

All the same, even after all these years, she still could not really understand it, although the passage of time had made the slight seem less. And she could not help feeling that with the senior partnership had come the patronising of Charles. Was it necessary to remind him, as often as he did, that it was he, Elliot, who had put Charles up for the Garrick and the Athenaeum? Was it kindness to introduce him – at Ascot, at Glyndebourne, at Wimbledon – as 'my Right-Hand Man?' They were no longer a part of it, but to Celia, Charles had seemed an outsider in the corporate world in which they lived.

Golf was another matter. Charles was a fine golfer, had played since boyhood and was a popular member of the Surrey club where he played and to which he subsequently introduced Elliot. Elliot, coming late to it, was slow to absorb the game's particular traditions and courtesies. More importantly, the low handicap he believed would provide his entrée to more prestigious clubs and clients eluded him. It was the first time he had set his sights on an objective and failed.

If it bothered Elliot that Charles was not only a better golfer but also a more popular competitor, he did not show it and after retirement they took to playing fourballs, joining a growing band of men who, all over England, on several mornings a week, set off with high hopes and battery-operated trolleys, defying age, weather and experience. At Monckton Heights, several members had died on the course, not from unusual exertion or a sudden, exciting return to youthful form, but simply because, as was agreed in the bar afterwards, their time had come. 'Damn fine way to go.' 'Just sunk a fifteen-footer for the match.' It was appreciated, if a member were planning to die on the course, that he should do so on the eighteenth or at least the seventeenth hole. Otherwise there was the problem of how to get old Rodway back from the twelfth or thirteenth, and whether everyone should abandon their matches and come in out of respect.

For years, while their children were growing up, the partners of Case and Millard had met, two or three times a year, for dinner or a weekend lunch in one of their homes. Celia remembered a time, shortly after her first miscarriage, when the occasion had been utterly and completely beyond her. She had hired caterers and passed it all off as her own, so that the legend had somehow grown that she was a Cordon Bleu cook. She wasn't, but it hadn't done her any harm. Her reputation told them that the food was wonderful even when their judgement told them otherwise. It was a bit like golf, she thought. If you had a good handicap, you could probably get away with some random shots.

Not all the partners, or indeed their wives, were still alive. But because Charles and Elliot played golf together every Sunday and Celia had acquired her reputation as a cook, lunch was nearly always at the Caves. The Wilsons were happy to come to her neat 1930's house conveniently situated between the golf course and the M4.

On the whole, she did not mind. She liked Angela, felt at home with her comfortable figure and lack of style. Elliot she could not stand. He had but to enter a room, tall, portly, with a sense of everything being stretched – the waistcoat over a perceptible stomach, the hair over a shiny head, the smile over a wide, untroubled face – for her nerves to jangle. And the irritating, the really galling thing was that he did not know, did not suspect, imagined that he carried her with him as he carried everyone else. She had never been able to dull, even momentarily, the patina of his self-esteem. She was grateful to him for occupying so much of Charles's time, but she found his impenetrability stifling. 'My dear Celia,' he would say, neck craning forward, head to one side, a half-smile playing about his lips, 'that was absolutely marvellous.' Every Sunday.

And every Sunday, when they brought the dishes through to the kitchen, he said the same thing: 'What shall I do with these?', holding out the dirty plates as if they were contaminated, like a surgeon disposing of swabs. 'Oh, just put them by the sink,' she said, week after week. It seemed too difficult, too much of a hurdle, to ask him to put them in the dishwasher. His whole projection said: 'Dishwashers? Don't understand them. Never deal with them.' She knew that if he had been asked, he would somehow have contrived to load them in such a way that they would have had to be taken out again, and re-stacked. He would have done it on purpose, but in such an artless, charming way that Charles, or Angela, or even she might have said, 'Poor old Elliot. Not of this world, is he?', Charles and Angela believing it.

And so she surprised herself last Sunday – yes, it was only last Sunday, if she dared to think about it – when he had come into the kitchen with his whimsical little half-smile and the pile of plates and she had suddenly, uncontrollably, snapped. She couldn't remember what exactly she had said. She hadn't sworn, she didn't think, but she remembered her head filling up with rage. She had turned and snatched the plates from his hands: 'Jesus Christ, Elliot'. Yes, that was what she had said, Jesus Christ Elliot. And she had taken the plates from him and hurled them at his feet, smashed them at his feet, by his feet, not actually on his feet – no, she hadn't done that – eight Wedgwood dinner plates, gravy and roast potatoes, sputtering into pieces on the terracotta floor.

And everyone rushing in. It seemed like everyone, it was only Charles and Angela. And Angela with her arm around Elliot saying, 'Are you all right, darling?', guarding him against her, the violent woman. And Charles blazing mad and saying, 'What in God's name?' and 'I'm so sorry, old man,' all in one breath. And the fussing over Elliot's shoes, Elliot's trousers,

Elliot's ego whilst she stood there, shaking, unable to cry, unable to leave the room.

'He's so bloody useless,' she screamed at Angela. 'No, I'm not round the bend,' as Charles, murmuring, sought to put his arm around her and draw her away. She elbowed her way out of his enclosure. 'I'm just sick to death of Elliot and his bloody posturing and the way we all give in to it, year after year. I'm sorry, Angela,' she said. Then she picked her way over the broken china and the gravy and went limply up to the bedroom, all passion spent. She cried, but they were the hot tears of anger and frustration and regret – not for what she had done, but for the way it was being interpreted. Even now, she could hear them making little sympathy noises, like wounded animals, in the kitchen.

'You'll have to apologise to Elliot.' Charles had come into the bedroom and was pacing about, agitated. 'We can't let them go home like this. I've made some coffee and they're in the drawing room. He's really being very good about it. Quite understands, totally out of character, women sometimes go off like that, and so on. Just say it's menopausal or something.'

'I'm not menopausal. I'm post-menopausal by about twenty years, if you remember. I just flipped. I just got ... fed up with him.' She opened a drawer and fumbled for a packet of cigarettes. Trembling, she took one out and put it to her lips. Charles lit it for her. They stood facing one another, Charles pleading, uncomprehending, she shaking, things flying round in her head, flying ...

'Please, darling. For me. Before it's too late.' He took the cigarette from her hand and ground it into an ashtray.

'Too late for what?'

'For ... everything', he said helplessly.

They were waiting for her in the drawing room, prepared and waiting, their faces turned towards her, bright, expectant, ready to register whatever emotion might be required.

'Elliot. I ... I'm so sorry. I don't know what came over me. One of those women's things. You know.'

'My dear'. He took her hands gently in his and led her to an armchair. 'I understand. I quite understand. There's really no need to explain. Coffee?' He had made himself perfectly at home again. He returned with the coffee, milk as she liked it, and the sugar bowl.

'One spoonful today, or two?' He smiled. 'Perhaps two.' He handed her the coffee, stirring it as he did so.

'And my dear. Did I tell you? The lunch was absolutely marvellous.'

Joseph Mueller's Gallery

She hurries out of the rain into the chapel and slips into a back pew, uncertain of the protocol. She had thought he was a Jew. Evidently not Orthodox or they would not now be in a crematorium. The service sheet is tucked inside the Book of Common Prayer. Really, she knows so little of his life. He sold her work. He had a wife, Rosa. He loved Mozart. She slips her wet raincoat off her shoulders…

I am the resurrection and the life, saith the Lord: he that believeth in me

and pushes it under the pew.

Though he were dead, yet shall he live

So few mourners. In the front, Rosa. Alone. Small in heavy overcoat and black, close-fitting hat. Outside, the rain continues.

We brought nothing into this world, and it is certain we can carry nothing out

'I could sell your work, if you would liven up your palette a bit.'
    His first words to her. Twenty-three, and at the end of her training. From art school in Glasgow to an MA at Camberwell. Proud of her work, uncertain of the future. Standing in her space at her School's Final Show, surrounded by her paintings. Urban landscapes, peopled by figures she has watched and sketched. Travellers on the underground. Women at bus stops. Men on park benches, under arches, in doorways. The isolation of urban life. '*Travailler beaucoup les effets du soir. Faire des groupes en pur silhouette au crépuscule.*' Degas. Her painting tends towards abstraction, her palette reflecting the masters she has studied and admired: Daumier, Millet, Goya, Manet. How she has loved the greys and the blacks.
    'I said …'
    'I heard what you said. Have you any idea,' she turns to face him, small features drawn, sharp Scottish voice rising, 'just how difficult painting is? Any idea at all?'

I will lift up mine eyes unto the hills from whence cometh my help

He never answered her question. He took from his breast pocket a wallet and from the wallet his card. Joseph Mueller, Art Dealer. Addresses in London and Munich. She knew his reputation.

'You must learn to think commercially. Any artist must, if she is to survive. I sell paintings to people who like something pleasant on their walls. They are prepared to pay good money.'

'Not all money is good.'

'And if your work doesn't sell?'

'If it doesn't sell, it doesn't sell.'

'How will you live?'

'Washing dishes. Waitressing. Whatever.'

'Ah well.' He turned to go. 'This,' he said, pausing before an oil of an old man, the only portrait amongst the landscapes, 'is very fine.'

Behold he that keepeth Israel shall neither slumber nor sleep

Friends and relatives, students and dealers, drift in and out of the exhibit. In the adjoining space, an artist talks about her work with text. Little fascinated groups lean towards intricate patterns of type. In the background, the low hum of video installations.

'Number fourteen. The price?'

A woman who visited her exhibit earlier, returning. Studying the portrait. 'I don't think you heard me. I asked how much the portrait is.'

'Yes, well....you see I'm not really sure, I mean I don't feel ...'

'I said: how much?'

Imogen consults the catalogue. 'Twelve hundred pounds. But the problem ...'

The woman is writing out a cheque.

'No, no. You don't understand. The painting is ...'

'Sold, I'm afraid.' Joseph Mueller has returned, taken a red 'sold' dot from Imogen's table, and placed it on the glass. The woman is aggrieved. The painting was in the catalogue, was clearly for sale, until two seconds ago had no red dot. Mueller apologises. He bought the painting earlier from the artist. Of course, they should have marked it. Could he interest her in another painting?

No. It was the portrait, the portrait particularly. It reminds the woman of her father.

Again, Mueller apologises.

So that the sun shall not burn thee by day, neither the moon by night

'It's my father.'
'I know. Here.' He is writing out a cheque.
'I can't sell it. That's what I was trying to explain.'
'Twelve hundred pounds. Expensive for an unknown artist. Still, you are right not to undervalue yourself.'
'A portrait of my father, painted shortly before his death – I hadn't imagined anyone would want to buy it. You don't, I'm sure. I won't take your cheque.'
'Actually you will. Our first transaction.' He looks at her. 'Amusing, is it not? I buy a painting which I give straight back to the artist. My business arrangements are normally more astute. Good afternoon.'
Placing the cheque on the table, he takes her card and leaves.

The Lord shall preserve thy going out, and thy coming in

Arriving at her studio at appointed times. Her studio in the small south London house, shared with other artists. His visits regular, carefully spaced. Places his umbrella in the stand, hangs up his hat, makes slow work of the stairs, holding the banister, a gold signet ring on his little finger. A fastidious middle-European gentleman. Once in her studio, indicating what he will take – no more than three or four paintings each visit – and she bringing them down, leaning them carefully against the wall by the door. A small but regular income. He took fifty per cent.

In my father's house are many mansions: if it were not so, I would have told you

He stayed never more than half an hour in all the – could it be fifteen? – years. Talked about her work, about music, about her family in Glasgow, about his wife Rosa, Jewish, deeply loved. Sometimes he asked for a tisane. When ready to leave, he called a cab. She took the paintings out to it whilst he stood holding open the door. He shook her hand and bowed, checking his breast pocket, making sure he had left the envelope with the cheque in it. Opening it later, she was surprised that the prices had been realised.

I am the way, the truth and the life

She never knew where her work went. Art fairs, he said, private clients, businesses. He spoke of a retrospective at some time in the future. It hadn't happened, and now it never would.

Now lettest thou thy servant depart in peace: according to thy word

She will say a few words to his widow

For mine eyes have seen: thy salvation

And then go home.

As it was in the beginning, is now, and ever shall be: world without end. Amen

Outside, sheltering in the porch, casting her eye down rows of rain-crushed wreaths, grouped according to the various deceased. None for Joseph Mueller. She, Imogen, has sent a donation, as requested in the newspaper, to the hospital that had nursed him at the last.

A hand on her shoulder.

'Imogen?'

'Oh', turning quickly, 'Oh. Mrs. Mueller...'

'Rosa, my dear. Rosa. Come back with me to the house. I would like you to. Come back with me in my car.'

Chauffeur-driven through rain and city traffic to the North London home. Narrow, dark, a single candle in the hallway, mirrors draped and covered.

'It is the custom, my dear, after a death. In the home, I am observant. Today is the first day of shiva, our seven days of mourning. We do not have flowers. We do not have wine and canapés. We remember the deceased, we honour him, we talk about him. We grieve. I will not leave the house now for the seven days. Joseph was not a Jew, but I do this for him.

'Come, my dear. Follow me. To the first floor.' Slowly, breathing erratically, mounting the stairs, Imogen following.

At the top, opening a door to the drawing room. A long room, well lit, hung with paintings. Every wall covered with paintings. Her paintings, Imogen sees at once. The paintings he has taken from her studio to sell.

'He … kept them?'

'Well …'

'He couldn't sell them?'

'He tried, my dear, he tried. He took them to the Art Fairs. He approached private clients. He thought it strange, since the first time he met you a woman had been mad for a portrait of your father. He said to me, 'Rosa. I must be losing my touch.'

'No,' I said, 'you have a good eye, Joseph. Is a matter of time, only. He thought perhaps it was the palette' – a twinkle in the tired brown eyes – 'a little sombre, he always said. Then after a time he stopped trying to sell them. 'Rosa', he said, 'I like these paintings. These paintings speak to me. These paintings are good for my soul.' And so he took down our Scottish colourists, our eighteenth century portraits, our English landscapes, and replaced them gradually with yours.'

They are all there. Every painting of Imogen's that he had chosen, and taken away – and paid her for. Tears begin to gather.

'Don't cry, my dear. Not for this. This he wanted to do. This he was happy to do. He had a daughter once, red-haired, like you.

'Later you must look around. You may choose any you would like to have, and take them away with you. It was his wish. I confess that I will miss them, but it was his wish.

'And now I would like you to sit with me a while. And we will remember my husband, and talk about his life…'

Not Another One

'You'll like Alan,' my Mum says.

'Yeah?' I say, staring at the screen. If she would just stop talking for a moment, I might get this finished.

'Yes. He's really nice. He loves kids.'

Not another one. They all love kids. Dote on them, apparently. Is she stupid or something? I move the cursor a centimetre to the right.

'You didn't say anything.'

'What?'

'I said, you didn't say anything.'

'What about?'

'Alan.'

'What Alan?'

'Alan who's my new boyfriend.'

Not another one.

He comes round on Sunday and Mum makes lunch. It's a peculiar meal with a sort of flat piece of grey meat – not a burger or anything recognisable – sitting in a pool of brown liquid with two potatoes and some peas. Also, it's summer, and we never have cooked lunch in the summer.

My mother, leaning towards him, says 'horseradish?' and he looks as if he's about to cry. He takes a little pot from her and puts something like Araldite on the side of his plate. 'Wonderful,' he says. 'I don't think I've had a real Sunday lunch since …' His voice trails off. He seems on the point of breaking up. My mother puts a hand on his arm in a tender gesture.

'Sssh,' she whispers, 'Sssh. I know. I understand.'

What are they *on*?

'We always have a roast on Sunday, don't we, Daniel?' my mother says to me, after a pause. The look on her face tells me I am supposed to agree, although I have no idea what she's talking about. 'Daniel loves it, don't you?'

'What?'

'The roast. You love it.'

I move the peas around in the brown pool. 'Yeah,' I say.

Alan, the lover of kids, is a hundred and two. I've worked that out. He has grey hair and two kids who are not kids any more but married with their own children, so he must be. My mother says the kids, the ones who are not kids, occurred in a previous relationship. She says previous relationship in a sort of whisper. He is very thin and tragic-looking, Alan, and quite tall. Taller than Peter Crouch, I should say. If my mother is going to have anyone round on Sunday, I'd sooner it was Peter Crouch.

'Well, Danny boy,' says this unfortunately-not-Peter Crouch, when he has finished his meal and wiped his mouth, 'Do you like school?'

In the first place, no-one calls me Danny, and certainly not Danny boy, and in the second place if he has any brains at all, he already knows the answer to that question.

'No,' I say, and get up and take my plate to the sink, en route to my computer.

'It takes a while,' I hear my mother saying, as I leave the room. I expect she is laying her hand on his arm in another tender gesture.

When I come down, to see what's on telly, Alan is at the sink. He has rolled up his sleeves and his arms are even thinner than I thought they would be, if I'd thought about them at all.

'Your mother is having a shower and washing her hair,' he says.

This is weird. Who has a shower and washes their hair in the middle of the afternoon?

'Why?'

He chooses not to answer that question but fills the sink with soapy water and starts to put the pans in. He is going to do the washing up, the creep.

At that moment my mum's mobile sounds off. It is very loud. 'Get that for me, Alan, would you,' my mother shouts from the top of the stairs.

'I'll get it,' I say and run to the sitting room. I take her phone out of the little pocket in her handbag and race back to the kitchen with it. Call me Usain Bolt.

'Catch!' I call to Crouch and lob the mobile to him before he has time to take his hands out of the soapy water and dry them. The phone lands with a splash and disappears into the bubbles.

'Omygod.' Crouch is fishing about in the soapy water. Mum is coming into the kitchen.

'Who was it?' she says, smiling at him and smelling like air freshener.

41

'Your son ...' Crouch begins, but I interrupt him.

'Alan dropped it in the water,' I say to her. 'He didn't mean to. It was an accident. Nobody's fault.' I give her one of my winningest smiles.

'Alan would like to take you to the fair,' my mother says, a week or so later, when she has recovered from the tragedy of the drowned mobile.

'Why?'

'He'd like to. He loves kids.'

'Would he like to take Paddy Donovan and Lloyd and Barry Cutler?'

'No.'

'Why not?'

'He'd like to take you. He'd like to get to know you.'

'Just me?'

'Well ... and me.'

'So he'd like to take you, and I drag along. Is that it?'

'Don't be difficult, Daniel.'

I love the Dodgems. The Dodgems are the best part of any fairground. Crouch agrees. He would like me to travel with him in his vehicle, but I come over all pathetic and say I want to go with my mum. My mum casts her eyes up to the sky but Crouch says, 'It's okay. I understand.'

Crouch has chosen his car – British Racing Green, he announces, like he's Lewis Hamilton or something – and is struggling into it. He seems to be trying to adjust the seat, which anyone who has ever been in one knows is impossible. He's put on a pair of spectacles. He has to wear glasses for driving, apparently.

There are warning notices, in capital letters, all round the rink. THIS WAY ROUND (with big white arrows for people who can't read). SEAT BELTS MUST BE WORN. NO CHILDREN AT THE WHEEL. NO HEAD-ON COLLISIONS. I settle down behind the wheel – my mother has given up at this point – the music starts, the overhead contacts begin to fizzle, and we're off. It's wicked. The screaming, the spinning, the smell of burning rubber. Round and round we go, biffing and dodging, dodging and biffing.

Each time Crouch overtakes us, he waves. Each time we overtake him, my mum waves back. He is showing off now, one hand on the wheel. He tries to overtake us on the inside and I seize my chance. I put my foot down, spin the wheel full circle and ram him in a head-on collision. His glasses jump off his face and on to the rink. Unfortunately my mum and I cannot avoid running over them.

Another Sunday and Crouch – spectacle-less – is round our house again. Only this time it's the evening, round about six. He is all done up in a suit.

'I thought we were going out.'

'We were. I'm sorry, Alan, I really am. I couldn't get a sitter.'

'I was looking forward to it.'

'I know. So was I. I tried everyone I could think of.'

'But ...'

'We'll have a nice time here. Really we will. There's plenty of wine and I've cooked us a lovely meal.'

I have seen a Marks and Spencer Ready Meal lurking by the microwave.

'But what about ...'

'I'll send him up to his room with a DVD. It'll be all right.'

'But ...'

'It'll be all right. Really it will.' She squeezes his hand.

I have my supper and watch TV for a while, then true to form Mum sends me upstairs with a DVD. She has laid the table with fancy napkins and little candles and is about to serve – I assume – the Marks and Spencer Ready Meal.

If you're going to send someone upstairs with a DVD you might find something more entertaining than The Tudors. I watch the porno bits, then come down to the sitting room, quietly, to look for another one.

Which is a waste of time because despite the early hour – it's only about nine – the sitting room is in darkness. They are on the sofa watching an episode of Desperate Housewives. I've seen it before, but it's a whole lot better than what I've got, so I creep across the room and settle down on the floor to watch it with them, behind the sofa.

We just get to a good bit when Crouch starts mumbling. He seems to be requesting something.

'Please, Linda, please ...'

'Not now, Alan ...'

'Please, darling. I've waited so long ...'

'Not now Alan ... Not here.'

'Why not? God you're beautiful. I want you so much.'

This could be Desperate Housewives, but on balance I think it's Crouch.

'Oh Alan. I can't. He might ...'

'He won't come down. He's upstairs in his room. It's all right. Darling ... darling...'

Crouch's not very interesting conversation peters out, and I can hear Desperate Housewives again. I start to pick up the story.

After a while Crouch begins to puff (he has never looked too fit). And now my mum is mumbling...

'Oh Alan. Oh God. Oh ... oh...' She sounds as if she might be about to die. Maybe she is about to die .....

I spring out from behind the sofa. 'Ta-da!'

Christmas time and my mum and I are in Tesco's – she hates Morrisons – doing the big shop. I drag along behind the trolley, popping items into it when she isn't looking. If it's only going to be her and me, I might as well have the things that I like. The store is very busy, stuffed with people. We circumnavigate the vegetables, and there, standing by the cheese counter, is Alan. He is with another woman and another kid.

'Alan!' I cry, and sprint over to the trio. 'Alan! Hey! How's it going?' I give him a High Five which, because he is not expecting it, lands somewhere in the middle of his stomach.

'Mum!' I wave to her, indicating my reunion with Crouch.

'Come here.' She is heading towards the exit, although we haven't bought anything.

'But ...'

'Come here this minute.'

'Why?'

'We're going to Morrisons.'

'But you hate ...'

'Daniel!'

I run to the exit. She takes me by the sleeve and drags me out.

'Who was that lady Alan was with?' I ask, as we head towards the car.

'Nobody.'

'Oh it was somebody, Mum. Alan called her something. Angela, I think it was. He called her Angela.'

'Angela Blackwell,' my mother says, through gritted teeth.

I wonder, for a moment, about running back and passing on to boy Blackwell a few of my tips. I decide against.
   Some things are best kept to oneself.

Christmas Letter

'I don't understand why you're doing it. You're just making yourself miserable.'

'We've always done it. Ever since we lived in Washington. If I miss out this year, people will think we're ill or something, and write. And I would have to write back. That would be worse.'

'Would it? You might find it easier to explain, in a personal letter.'

'Tom. I can't ever explain it. Not to you, not to Justine, not to myself. Can you?'

'No. Sorry, Mum.' He flicked off the television and walked round the table to where his mother was sitting in front of her laptop. She looked small, small and hunched over her small screen, brown hair caught back in a pink plastic comb, absurdly matching her cardigan. He saw the heading: *Christmas Letter 2012.* 'What a bloody farce,' he said, and taking an apple from the fruit bowl, went out of the room.

She heard his bedroom door close behind him. The tears she had been holding back dropped on to the backs of her hands. She watched them run over the skin, the incipient age spots. She clenched her fingers, and they ran off faster.

She brought up *Christmas Letter 2011* and opened the text. 'It has been a good year for the Donnellys, or should we say a lucky one', it began cheerily. 'Justine, having just missed her projected A Level grades of 2 As and a B, nevertheless secured a place at Leeds to read History of Art next October. (She said it was the interview that clinched it. Must have inherited some of the Donnelly blarney!). She now plans the mandatory Australasian back-packing tour during her year out, so may we take this opportunity of saying to the Watsons in Sydney and the Hamiltons in Melbourne and any other friends who may find themselves on her itinerary: Don't say you haven't been warned! Tom did well in his GCSEs and has started A Levels at the local Sixth Form College. He had planned to take Maths, Physics, Chemistry and Biology but after a few weeks (to the relief of his father, who was worried about the workload) decided to sub-stitute Higher Maths for Biology.' (Really, she thought, did anybody care).

She read on. Yes, it had been a good year. Joe had been given tenure in the Department of Metallurgy (at Birmingham still); Kate, now that the children were more or less off her hands, had taken up her silk-screen printing again; Jean, Joe's mother, had moved into sheltered accommodation in Solihull and Bella had survived a road accident which, sadly, had left her lame in one leg. The vet had done a wonderful job, but it had taken a long time for the break to heal.

It seemed, too, that their friends must be interested in a year in the life of their house, for she read that its outside had been painted, its basement converted into a workshop-cum-rumpus room ('somewhere for the kids to hang out'), that its boiler had broken down ('on the coldest day of the year') but had been replaced. Their house, it seemed, like some elderly relative, had by care and repair somehow been kept going and, God willing, would hang on for a few years yet. Well, Americans always keep you up to speed on the state of their homes. In summer the decking is replaced and in winter the storm windows go up – always only just in time.

She thought about the 'voice' of the letter, the curious convention of the omniscient author who is supposed to be anonymous but who in fact is immediately identifiable. This year, departing from their convention, the voice would be hers, of course. In the past, it had always been Joe's.

She had addressed the envelopes, eighty of them. When you have lived abroad you accumulate a large number of friends and they are friendships that continue down the years, whatever alterations may occur. Or so she hoped.

'Getting anywhere?' Tom was looking in on his way out to the pub.

'Not really.'

'I still think it's odd, sending out letters of sad tidings.'

'It's not pleasant, but it has to be done.'

'You don't have to do it at all.'

'I think I do. And I've told you why. By the way' (as he turned to go) 'if you felt like helping me put some of them in envelopes later on it'd be a help.'

'How many?'

'Eighty.'

'Christ. I'm not doing eighty.'

'I didn't mean the whole lot. Just a few, if you have a moment.'

'I might. When I come in.'

'Dear friends,' she typed. 'This letter is as hard for me to write as I imagine it will be for you to receive, in that our family has suffered a sea change since we wrote to you at the end of last year. Nonetheless we want to wish you all a very happy Christmas and health and good fortune in the coming year.

'To start with the constants in our lives, our children. Justine has started her degree course at Leeds. She is living in halls of residence and seems happy. She has a new boyfriend, Sam, whom we have not met but she – or perhaps both of them – will descend on us sometime during the next week, when term ends. She plans to waitress in the holidays to finance a ski-ing holiday after Christmas (this may turn out to be a pipe-dream). Tom, who at six foot two now towers over Joe, is in the Upper Sixth and having a career-choice crisis'. She deleted 'having a career-choice crisis' and went on: 'and is currently undecided whether to apply to study medicine or veterinary science. If the latter, he wonders if it was wise to have dropped biology. He is not getting much help either from the college or from his father. However, he is very grounded (I think that's the right phrase!) and I'm sure will make the right choice. I only hope we can afford it. Tuition fees have gone up enormously.

'In February our beloved labrador Bella had to be put down and Joe – to cheer me up, I think – suggested I go with him to Cracow, where he was lecturing to the European Congress of Mineral Sciences. Whilst we were there, we were approached by a Polish post-graduate student who wanted to do her Ph.D. at Birmingham, in Joe's department. She hoped that Joe would be her supervisor. Joe doubted that he could find the money to fund her, but when we got back there was a letter saying that she had arranged funding with a Polish research institute and could start at Birmingham in May. She arrived in April and quickly integrated into the department. Apparently she is an out-standing student. I'm afraid I failed to read the signs and so was shattered when Joe announced that he was moving out and into a faculty flat where she now lives with him. We still hope that this may be an infatuation and that he will come back to us. The children are much affected but have been immensely supportive to me, especially Tom who of course is still at home.

48

'Please keep in touch and visit when you can. Our home remains open to you, as always.

The Donnellys
Kate, Justine and Tom,
Hillside,
December 2012.'

She pushed her chair away from the table and leant back. The letter had been typed quickly, without pause. Tomorrow she would read it through and see if it could be sent.

Tom, coming in past midnight and seeing the screen still lit, sat down heavily in front of it. He read the letter through and went back to the penultimate paragraph. Taking the cursor, he scrolled to 'and so was shattered when Joe...' highlighted the remainder, deleted it, and typed in 'fucked off.'

He switched on the printer, commanded PRINT 80, and waited for the pages to feed through.

The Dinner Party

'A little domestic incident, darling,' her mother said. 'That's what you need. It makes the evening go with a swing. Eases the tension. People don't like coming into a home and finding everything perfect, it makes them feel uneasy. The perfect is the enemy of the good. Someone said that, a philosopher, I think. French. I don't know how I know that because on the whole I can't stand the French. But it's true. Your father used to get irritated with me. 'Oh don't do that spilt milk-bottle thing again,' he would say. But it was only a little bottle – well it was a big bottle but only a little milk. They hear a crash in the kitchen and me crying out: Oh my God! And then I sail in saying: Silly me. There's goes tomorrow's breakfast. And everyone laughs. 'Are you all right?' 'Oh fine. It didn't take a moment to wipe up.' Nor did it. We gave the most successful dinner parties. Mind you, milk doesn't come in bottles any more, so that's out.'

It is Carina's first dinner party for Brian. Their first formal dinner party. He is currently unaware of her mother's curious recipe for social success and this is just as well. He is already nervous about the evening. It could be the making of him. On the other hand, if it's a fiasco he's yesterday's man. He knows what it feels like to be yesterday's man, he's been there. But this is a new company and a new start. And Carina a new wife. He met her in a club at the end of a divorce and the beginning of a plan to play the field again, but to play it more strategically. She was more or less what he was looking for, young, pretty, not career driven, as Tara had been. Not given to unpredictable, alcohol-fuelled excesses of language and behaviour. A nice girl, the right sort. The sort, if not actually to further, at least not to obstruct a husband's plans for his future.

'What we need,' he'd said, steadying his beer on the bar, 'is some posh totty. Something in the Zara Phillips line.'
    'Well we're not going to find it here.'
    'No. We'll have to raise our game. Spend some roubles. Find out where it's happening. Where it's at. Put ourselves about a bit. Start drinking vodka cocktails.'
    'Bloody hell.'
    'As ye sow so shall ye reap.'
He hadn't fancied her at first. Hadn't really noticed her, if the

truth be told. Pete was chatting her up. It was when he heard her surname that he kicked into gear. Or rather, when he heard her explaining her surname. Anyone whose surname was pronounced differently from the way it was spelled had to be worth a second look.

She went off to powder her nose. She actually said it, powder her nose.

'Way to go,' he said. 'Featherston ... what was it?'

'Featherstonhaugh. Pronounced Fanshaw.'

'Bloody hell. But posh, right?'

'Like you'd go around with a name like that if you weren't. Anyway, all yours.'

'Doesn't do it for you?'

'Nah. Too young. And a bit... '

'A bit what?'

'I don't know ... a bit vacant. And stout.'

'I can learn to love stout.'

She came back from powdering her nose looking somehow less stout, and Brian moved in.

Roger Featherstonhaugh, pronounced Fanshaw, had been a stockbroker. That was where the family lived, in the belt. His widow was small, round, purposeful, a little spitfire of a woman. She had no idea why the surname was pronounced as it was. 'Haven't a clue,' she told Brian, when he asked her. She had once been quite interested in her husband's family, but had received no encouragement. She said there was a castle up in Northumberland but that was some other part of the family. Nothing to do with us, Roger said. She had thought they might drive up and have a look at it sometime, but Roger had always put it off.

'Such a shame,' she said. 'I looked it up on the internet. There's a lovely coat of arms. *Valens et Volens*. Able and willing. Jolly good motto, I always think.'

'Made for you, Mummy.'

'I know. I should have been born a Featherstonhaugh.'

'I don't see why not,' she said, when Brian asked for her daughter's hand in marriage. 'The fact that you made a mess of the first one should mean you pay a little more attention to the second. Are you on good terms with your ex-wife?'

'I'm afraid not.'

'That's good. I don't believe in this amicable divorce nonsense. And Carina tells me there are no children?'

'That's right.'

'Excellent. I think she should be all right, provided there isn't some irritating first wife hanging around in the background.'

'There won't be.'

'Good. Carina's a sweet girl, lovely daughter, but a bit woolly.'

'Woolly?'

'You know, a bit vague. I sometimes feel she's on a different planet. Marriage will be good for her, bring her down to earth. I have to tell you, I don't like your name.'

'Parker?'

'No, not Parker. Nothing wrong with Parker. It's a bit pedestrian, but there's nothing wrong with it. It's the Brian bit.'

'I can't help that.'

'Life of Brian. It's a sort of joke. Haven't you any other names?'

'Brian Charles.'

'What a funny family.'

'Why?'

'Getting them the wrong way round. Charles is so much nicer. I might call you Charles.'

'I hope you won't.'

Sometimes she did and sometimes she didn't. There was no knowing. Mrs. Featherstonhaugh behaved quite unlike anyone Brian had ever met, certainly unlike anyone with such a long name was supposed to behave.

In the middle of the wedding preparations, the mother of the bride decided to sell her house.

'Why on earth?' Brian asked.

'She says: why not? Everything's decided, the reception's not at the house, she doesn't want a lot of awful people staying during the wedding, and the estate agent's got someone who's interested.'

'She should go into sheltered housing or move to Malaga or do something mothers-in-law are supposed to do.'

'She doesn't want to. Why should she? She's active.'

'Too active. And why London? Why doesn't she stay where she is? Elderly people are supposed to live in villages.'

'She doesn't like villages. She's gone off them. She wants to be in the city.'

'Pity the city.'

'And go to classes. And learn to salsa.'

'Ridiculous.'

'That's what she said.'

'Your mother is beyond eccentric.'

Mrs. Featherstonhaugh sold her house, and the couple married, in the Spring. In the summer they bought a rather impressive Tudor style house near the park, on the back of Carina's legacy from her father. It is now early Autumn. The dinner party guests, among them Brian's chairman Sir John Anderton and his wife, will arrive as the light is failing but in time to be impressed by the circular drive, imaginatively landscaped and lit.

'I've never really done a dinner party,' Carina said, when he'd mooted it.

'You must have.'

'No, not really. Suppers. I've done suppers. Pasta and stuff, like we have here.'

'What about when you lived in a flat with the girls? You were always asking blokes round to dinner – or so you told me.'

'It wasn't dinner as such. We didn't know what we were doing. We'd buy a chicken on the way home and ring up Mummy to find out what to do with it.'

'Oh god.' How could someone so well bred be so useless? 'We'll have to get in caterers.'

'Cool.'

'And someone to waitress. You can't be upping and downing all the time. You need to be at the table.'

'Okay.'

'Do you know someone who can waitress? Someone presentable, you know, with a nice voice. Not estuary.'

'Not offhand, but Mummy will. Or if she doesn't, she'll find someone.'

'And by the way, when you introduce them, it's Sir John and Lady Anderton.'

'I know.'

'And you don't introduce them to other people, you introduce other people to them.'

'I know.'

'Don't call him John. He might invite you to but he won't mean it. He's not the type. His wife might, she might mean it. She's quite a nice old bean. She might say: Violet, please, and you might use it once or twice. Not too much. It's safer to go back to Lady Anderton. And...' (remembering Tara) 'don't drink.'

'I don't drink much,' Carina said.

'I know you don't. But don't drink at all. Just raise the glass to your lips and put it down again. Like the Queen.'

'Great evening.'

'Yes, it should be a great evening, entertaining important people in our own home. It is important, you know, this dinner party, Carina. Important to me.'

'I know. I just wish it was over.'

Finally she focussed, got a grip. The table is laid, the caterers are in the kitchen, Samantha has arrived to serve and has passed the test, has a nice voice and no face-piercings. Mrs. Featherstonhaugh has stopped telephoning offering advice. The house is looking lovely, bowls of flowers everywhere. Carina is a whiz with flowers. She took a course in it after she left school. She checks a bowl in the hall, bending to smell them, to cup them in her hands and let them fall a little less formally. Everything detailed but everything casual, natural, welcoming. She knows the form. He doesn't have to worry.

The phone rings. Casually, she picks it up.

'What? Oh No. Oh God. How awful. Yes, yes of course.'

Brian is at her side, agitated, pacing.

'Not Sir John? Not cancelling?'

'No.' She puts down the receiver. 'It's Mummy.'

'Jesus.'

'She's been in a pile-up on the Westway.'

'Dead?'

'No, not dead. Not hurt, actually. But the car's a write-off and she's disorientated. They need a next of kin.'

'No, Carina...'

But she has thrown on her coat, whipped the car keys off the hook and dashed out of the door. She jumps into the car, starts up the engine and speeds out of the drive as Sir John and Lady Anderton's Bentley makes its way in. The chauffeur swerves to avoid her. She toots and gives a wave of thanks. And is surprised to see Sir John and Lady Anderton, puzzled, waving back.

Closing Down

Life as she knew it came to an end when Woolworths closed. She stood outside the store in her clear plastic raincoat, the first drops of rain beading its surface, and looked down the street she had lived in, shopped in, loved in (her first date, in the corner café, with a boy from the caravan site) and might even die in – yes, even that – and she wondered what had happened to it all.

It used to be a lovely street, the high street. It used to have shops the descriptions of which were now more or less extinct. A confectioner. A milliner (did anyone today know what a milliner was?). A gentlemen's outfitter and a ladies' one as well, where you could buy your stockings and your underwear. A jeweller where you could get your watch repaired. A bakery which sold the best doughnuts in Lincolnshire. A tea shop and a corner café, two newsagents and a hairdresser, a shoe shop, a wool shop, a luggage shop. She had used every one of them, except the luggage shop. She and Charlie had never needed any luggage because they had never been anywhere. Not overnight. And why should they, living close to the sea like they did? It used to be a little world, the high street. Her world. And look at it now.

Mind you, there were shops where she had felt less comfortable than others. The ladies outfitter, for instance. Jennings. She hadn't been sorry to see that go, as long as she could still get her underwear in Woolworths. Jennings sold beautiful clothes, of course, tweed skirts and knits, tailored suits and silk blouses. Cashmere. She knew that it served a different sort of woman, the sort of woman she tried hard to avoid when she popped in for her stockings and her cross-your-heart bra. She heard their voices: 'Have it sent up to the house, would you Mr. Patrick.' She wondered what it was that prevented them from carrying their own shopping home. Of course, Madam. Certainly Madam. With her, it was sometimes Madam, sometimes Mrs. Sutherland, more often Nancy. Not that it bothered her. She didn't go to the high street to be fawned upon. She went to get what she needed and to feel her world around her.

The wool shop went before the jewellers. Charlie said she shouldn't worry, it wasn't as if they needed the money. Which was true, except that a little extra always comes in handy, but what he didn't understand was that it wasn't the money. It was knowing that a customer had gone into the shop with a pattern, and bought the wool and needles and asked Mollie Hammond if she had anyone who could knit it up for her, and Mollie Hammond answering that yes she had, and she would give her knitter a ring, and she would knit it up lovely and she was sure madam would be pleased. It was nice to be known as something, as a knitter. It made her feel proud.

Some time before it closed, before Mollie Hammond had seen her in the street and told her she couldn't make a living from it any more, some time before that she had started getting orders involving dark colours, black and navy. 'It's what people are going in for these days,' Mollie Hammond said. 'Horrible, to my mind. I like a bit of colour.'

She found she was beginning to have headaches. The three-ply navy cable nearly finished her. Charlie bought her a standard lamp, an offer from a Sunday newspaper. The Brita-Lite. Banish Eye Strain Forever. He said he hoped it would help. It did, a little, but not enough, and so they sent it back. It had a 28-day return policy on it. 'Just don't take on any more of them dark colours,' Charlie said. 'You won't, will you?' She said she didn't know, she wasn't in a position to pick and choose. In any case, she liked to knit.

'I think you should give it up, love. I don't like to see you, your eyes screwed up like that.' And when he touched her face, and said he worried about her, she told him not to be soft, and cried a little. If only they'd had children, grandchildren. Pinks, blues, yellows, lilacs. She could have gone on knitting for ever.

Charlie said she should get it sorted, because she was ruining her sight. Sorted was a word Charlie liked a lot, Charlie and his brother Reg. Because that's what they did, sorting, every morning, 6 a.m. when the delivery vans arrived. They sorted the fruit and the vegetables and laid them out in neat, cantilevered rows, like theatre seats, in front of the shop. They looked a picture, on the artificial grass. And they threw away the rotten ones, they were known for it, Charlie and Reg, you never found a bad apple or a wet onion in your bag. It had been the same with their father. They were good lads, the Sutherlands. You could trust them. They'd struggled first with decimalisation and then with metric, though they still had scales in the back of the shop for pounds and ounces. And when things began to get tougher, and the rates went up, they had started with health foods – nuts and so on – and a few garden plants. Organic they weren't interested in, didn't even think about. People round here, they didn't have the money for organic. And for a while the few extras they were offering made a difference. But then the rates went up again and the new superstore opened down by the leisure centre and there were days when Charlie didn't feel so dusty. So reluctantly, because they both enjoyed the trade, they decided to pack it in. Everyone missed them. Everyone said so. But would those everyones have been enough to keep them going?

The bakery had stopped baking. They bought in now, from Louth. Fresh. Delivered every morning. But somehow it wasn't the same. And the doughnuts had gone. No call for them, apparently. How you would measure a call for doughnuts, she couldn't imagine. If they were there, you bought them. There were never any left by lunchtime.

By the time she got inside the store she'd forgotten what it was she'd come for and had come away with two pillows which she hadn't wanted, 20% off. You would have expected more, wouldn't you, with the closing down and all. 20% was not what she would call Prices Slashed. Really, she didn't need them, and the bags were heavy and bulky in the wet. She shifted them from one hand to the other. If she was one of these modern people she would be on her mobile telling Charlie to come down and give her a hand.

The government should have stepped in. The government should have saved it. Someone should have written to Tony Blair, or that Mr. Brown. It had been a place to socialise, Woolworths, a place for everyone. The young went in for their CDs. The children for their pencils and sweets. The mums for school uniforms. The dads for paint and DIY. And Nancy. Nancy just went in. For the comfort of it. And she might be in the towels, or the tableware, or the birthday cards, when 'Fancy seeing you here! Lovely day, isn't it. Have you heard about …' And the aisles would take up and absorb the gossip, muffled by the height of them, by the socks and the clothes and the table-ware, by the music and the pick 'n' mix.

It was a big store. It occupied three frontages of their small high street. It would leave a big hole. A hole Charlie didn't expect to see filled. Not in his lifetime.

Charlie. He'd wanted her to wait until the boiler man had been. But 'I need to get there early. It's the last day,' she'd said. He had helped her on with her raincoat and kissed her at the door. 'Don't you worry,' she'd said. 'I'll be all right.' She knew he didn't like her being out on her own.

She hurried up the street, past the two bookmakers and the charity shops, past the Chinese Takeaway and the new wine bar, past the shoe shop. Shoenique. Racks of high-heeled boots, stacks of shiny black wedges, baskets of trainers. Closing Down. Last Few Days. It had been having its last few days for as long as she could remember. From the day it opened, she shouldn't wonder.

Once it had been the butcher's. Meat hooks, now painted white, still hung from the ceiling, above the racks of shoes. What had been the name? She remembered the striped awning and above it the blue letters, edged with gold, on a white tile background. But what did they say? She should be able to remember the butcher, surely. She screwed up her eyes and stared into the shop, not seeing young Tracey Chapman, waving, at the till. For a moment she thought she had it. It danced about at the edges of her consciousness, and was gone. Charlie would remember. He would know. And he would tell her that she mustn't fret. That everyone forgets things once in a while. That she could remember words like milliner, and if you could remember a word like milliner, there couldn't be much wrong.

She set her face against the rain and pushed on up the street.

The Necklace

When my mother died, it was her jewellery that bothered me. Even to touch it seemed sacrilegious, so much a part of her had it become.

'You must deal with your mother's effects.' Her solicitor telephoned me several times a week, making me feel very childish and very hopeless. And indeed hopeless is what I was for I had lost the last of my blood relatives and for a time I felt quite unconnected to the human race.

My mother's effects. So strange a phrase, and strangely appropriate. For my mother was, above all, an effect. She dressed for effect, she was witty for effect, she was effective with her friends, often turning their lives around in ways which they could never have anticipated nor in some cases, desired. She was blonde, bold, glitzy, glamorous. Think Marlene Dietrich, Tallulah Bankhead, Mae West. She was ostrich feather and cocktail hat, pencil skirt and long cigarette holder. If ever there was a woman who personified the Forties when, with your husband alive (just) and returned from the war, life was to be taken on the run – lest it should disappear again – it was my mother. The story of the jewels began in Cairo.

'Darling.' My father's letter had been written in the desert. His neat handwriting veered, here and there, from its path, where the table legs had slipped in the sand. 'We were in Cairo again this afternoon. I have found the most marvellous jeweller. He is making a ring for you to celebrate the first anniversary of our wedding. It is a stone which you have not favoured in the past but it caught my eye in the window – in fact I think it winked at me – and it was so stunningly beautiful I knew it was for you. We discussed the setting and I think he has a picture of you in his mind and will do it, and you, justice. It comes with all my love and longing. Your own, James.' My father used to write letters like that to my mother. I would dig them out of her bottom drawer on rainy days and try to associate them with the cheerful, middle-aged man who was my father. Actually, that is not true. Or only half true. I drew back from making that final connection, preferring to think of these star-crossed lovers as some couple other than my parents. Children are like that. At the bottom of this embarrassing letter was a postscript: 'The ring will arrive in a scent bottle.'

I can see now, of course, that he hadn't meant a scent bottle, but the box, into which both scent and ring had been packed. But as a child I used to imagine my mother smashing the bottle on the floor to release the ring from its exotic reservoir. In Cairo, my father told me, you didn't go into a shop and buy a bottle of ready-packaged perfume. Oh no. You found a little man (my father's world was full of little men), a perfumier, who would blend mysterious oils and spices in secret recipes to suit the particular allure of a particular woman. He was good at his job, I'd say. Because although, like Monroe, my mother always declared herself a Chanel No. 5 girl, no perfume was ever so much 'her' as the one in that green and gold cut-glass bottle, still breathing faintly (or do I imagine it?) after more than half a century. So I suppose that's what my father did, the old romantic, had the jeweller run to the perfumier (or the other way round) and pop the ring into the box before it was sent off.

When people talk about the North Africa Campaign, they probably see officers in pale khaki and long socks and pink knees poring over maps in tents. Whereas what I see is little men in Tommy Cooper fezes (I don't know why) running through the dark alleyways of Cairo with precious gems and perfumes which, on the command of my father, were to be fired off in small boxes to his bride of less than one year, my mother. The ring was a ruby. I know this, because sometimes my father would say: 'You never wear the ring I had made for you in Cairo.' And my mother would reply: 'It doesn't quite go with what I'm wearing, darling.' Or, 'I was wearing it yesterday, but you didn't notice.' Neither of which was true. 'I hate rubies,' my mother once said to me. She said it sotto voce, as if it mattered.

I never saw the ring, but I saw the stone. My mother might wear a piece of jewellery, a necklace or a brooch, for some years, and seem quite devoted to it, until one day the stones would suddenly and surprisingly reappear as something else. The ruby became the eye of a cat in an otherwise marcasite brooch. She had seen something similar on a lapel of Wallis Simpson, although I can't believe that Wallis Simpson's eye was red. In fact, I can't believe in Wallis Simpson's cat. Perhaps it was a panther. As far as I know, she hated cats, domestic cats. She liked those horrible little dogs, those pugs.

All this 'setting,' this passion my mother shared with a woman for whom a king gave up a throne, involved exciting, often clandestine ('it's best your father doesn't know') visits to an old, yellowing man in a shop that had iron grilles across the window, and padlocks, and who wore dress shirts without the collar and a waistcoat and thick, protruding glasses which stuck out from his eyes like reverse binoculars. These were not as scary to a child as you might imagine, for I had the distinct impression that actually he could not see me at all, and I believe that I was right.

'Hes Medam a new fentasy for me?' Mr. Engelsman would ask, his voice sparkling. I could tell you that his eyes sparkled – but how would I know? You have to believe that something sparkled in Mr. Engelsman when my mother walked into his shop, not just because I'm telling you, but because that's the way it was.

'Medam's sepphires are ready.' Sometimes Mr. Engelsman would telephone the house, and if my father answered he was more than likely to be angry, for of course it was he who had bought the original piece which had now, like post-war territory, been redistributed. 'But darling. I thought you loved the bracelet.' And then my mother would launch into her rearguard defence. I remember that she would use the words surprise, economical and jewellery a lot, unaware that in most people's minds only two of them go together. My father capitulated (what choice did he have?). I always knew that, for her, he would have given up a throne.

In fact, my mother didn't like sapphires either. She thought they had been over-worn by the royal family. She really only liked emeralds and diamonds and pearls. And those sapphires, which worked so hard for her, as necklace, brooch, bracelet and dress clips, have their final resting place in a piece of such eccentricity I treasure it still. My mother had visited a friend in hospital – I think it was the only time she ever was in a hospital – and seen Sister's watch, pinned to the breast of her stiff white apron. She was entranced, and Mr. Engelsman engaged forthwith to produce a small, square fob-watch which pins to the dress behind a sapphire bow. It has one defect, unnoticed in the making either by Mr. Engelsman or his muse. The face does not hang upside down, as it should, and so can be read only by someone not wearing it.

I wonder, had she lived, whether she would have re-designed the necklace, the necklace which my father gave her on their fortieth wedding anniversary and which had necessitated more than one weekend in London and several visits to the Burlington Arcade. I think not. It was the finest piece of jewellery she ever possessed, seven strands of tiny seed pearls barred by small, rather milky, light green emeralds with darker emeralds and diamonds at the drop. Even I, who am not much interested in jewellery, found it ravishing. It was old, and had been part of a great collection, now broken up. 'Wallis Simpson?' I asked. My mother sniffed. No, it didn't look Wallis Simpson. It looked … Anna Karenina, the Imperial balls, the Winter Palace, the frozen Neva. So I gave it a history. I was studying the Romanovs at the time, and cut out from a book a photograph of the ballerina Kschessinska who, before her marriage, had been the mistress of Nicholas II. She did not at all resemble my mother and had rather gappy teeth, which was a disappointment to me, but I had settled on her by now. I wrote in the sepia ink my grandfather used to use. I thought it looked more authentic: 'Magnificent 19th century necklace of pearls, diamonds and emeralds. Made by the House of Fabergé for the Tsarevich Nicholas as a gift for Mathilde Kschessinska. St. Petersburg, 1892.' I gave it to my mother, who laughed with delight and folded it and slipped it very carefully under the lid of the box.

And so it was that I brought myself finally to deal with my mother's effects. For the last time I took the case that contained the necklace, holding the soft leather in both my hands, pressing the brass release which let the lid swing slowly open, the milk-white and emerald brilliance sparkling in the satin. I had never worn it. She had offered to lend it to me once, for a ball, but it was always too grand for me. I ran my hand over it. 'Real pearls are always warm,' she used to say. She believed in real things, real jewels, real fantasies.

I took the necklace to a London auction house. An expert was called. He was young, and not at all like Mr. Engelsman. He held the necklace out and turned it this way and that in the light. 'It could be Fabergé. The fact that it is set in platinum gives credence. No mark existed in Russia for stamping platinum, so that many pieces like this one left his workshop unmarked. And this?' He held up my attribution.

  'Oh, just an old piece of paper. Pay no attention to it.'
  'On the contrary, it's not unreasonable. Kschessinska was the

recipient of many gifts from the Romanovs, not only from Nicholas, but from the Grand Duke Sergei and the Grand Duke Andrei, whom she later married. She was still alive in Paris in the Sixties, you know. It should be possible to find out.'

In fancy's maze we sometimes stoop to truth. Some months later correspondence with the auction house was concluded. The piece was catalogued: 'Magnificent 19th century necklace of pearls, diamonds and emeralds. Made by the House of Fabergé for the Tsarevich Nicholas as a gift for Mathilde Kschessinska. St. Petersburg, 1892.' And sold, far exceeding the reserve.

Emperor of the Pool

The pool is beautiful now, from where he sits in his chair on the ten meter board. The water is almost still, lapping only gently against the sides from the strokes of the few elderly swimmers doing their wide, old-fashioned breaststroke and feeble freestyle in designated lanes. The not-quite turquoise, not-quite green paint of the pool's skin presents the water in an altogether attractive light, so that you might forget the chlorine and the things that get caught up in the filter system and the number of kids who might have peed in it that morning, when the schools were in, and think of the South of France and Dufy or California and Hockney and all those little pools you see from the air when you are coming in to land over Athens or Malaga or even, nowadays, Surrey. Little touches of blue, like kingfishers' wings. Transient birds, transient wealth but while it lasts a private pool says exclusivity and real estate and impossibly beautiful people stretching long, bronzed limbs along impossibly comfortable pool furniture. They lie there, these beautiful people, miraculously protected against melanoma without benefit of Total Block or Factor Fifteen, sipping long, colourful drinks which in other circumstances – Sunday morning down the Flower and Firkin, for example – might even be considered naff. A private pool cushions you from all that, the naffness and discomfort of hot summer days.

The lifeguard adjusts his position in his seat on the high diving board. He sits in it at an angle, thin legs apart, torso slightly slumped. He pulls the white tee-shirt away from his body in an attempt to introduce some air to his chest and armpits, but the wet cotton quickly finds his body again. The words, in orange capitals, POOL ATTENDANT, fold into the creases of the garment and he is glad, for Pool Attendant seems an inadequate description of the responsibility a job like his involves, sitting up here, gazing down, people's lives in his hands. You cannot afford to slack off, not for an instant, drowning happens so quick. He remembers the morning that little kid jumped in. Straight out of the changing room and into the water, his mother running screaming after him. His whistle had brought Mr. Bloxham on the scene and it was suddenly all poolside first-aid, and recovery positions, and mouth-to-mouth, although not all of this was strictly necessary. Mr. Bloxham had got the glory, of course, but the Pool Manager had praised him too, saving a little lad's life and the council a lot of money and bad publicity. 'You done good, kid,' he'd said. The mother had decided to sue anyway, on the grounds that there weren't any railings between the changing room and the pool. There were now.

The reason the lifeguard is sitting on the high diving board is that all the boards, including the high springboard, are closed to the public following an incident where a child jumped off the high springboard and landed on an old lady, breaking her back. It would have been funny if it hadn't been so awful. At first they had forbidden jumping from the high boards. Diving only, on the assumption that you were more likely to look where you were going if you went in head first. It hadn't worked. You can't stop kids running and jumping and not looking where they're going. Not once they get up on the high board. A kind of madness overtakes them. It has to do with the splashing and the shouting and the echoing and the feeling that they are no longer in their own bodies. There's a moment when they could stop, but it's always the moment after the die has been cast and they are spilling off the board and into the pool like hand grenades, screaming as they fizz down into the water. The risk is against their own fear, against being found, alone, shivering on the high board when everyone else has gone, the only way down the disgrace of the steps.

He likes it up here. It's better than being by the poolside. He feels powerful, remote, a king, an emperor. Emperor of the Pool, although he realises how foolish this might sound to anyone else, his family, the pool lads, the girl in the green frilly swimsuit. He is surprised what a turn-on that swimsuit is. Normally he likes bikinis. But there is something about the way the colour darkens, to a sort of emerald, when she jumps into the water, the way the costume moves with and against her body, like weed.

She generally comes in about three, which makes it hard to figure out much about her. Too late for lunch and too early to have knocked off work. Always on her own. She is posh, he feels sure of that. Not all-the-vowels Range Rover posh, just out-of-his-league posh. It has something to do with the way she moves, for he has never heard her voice. All the same, he doesn't half fancy her. But what can he do, the distance between them is so great.

She is one of the reasons for his presence at the pool, in a job which is not well paid and which, his mother says, has no prospects. His mother feels she is seeing three years of art college go to waste. She doesn't understand how the job suits his mood just now. It gives him time to think, produces a sort of reverie. He is in a limbo between education and the world, and the world, he feels, is better kept at a distance for the present. He isn't ready for it and it probably isn't ready for him. Actually, it is unaware of his existence. It's the same with the girl.

She has come in now. She is in the water, playing with the water. She is doing it again. That thing she does. Sinking to the bottom of the pool, sculling with her hands, working against the water's buoyancy. Down she goes, her hair streaming upwards and now here it comes, the frill of her bathing costume, following her hair like a sea anemone. She is right down now, crouched on the bottom of the pool. She sits there, like a lambent sea creature, the fronds of her hair and her frill settling around her, only her hands playing against the water, keeping her down. She waits a moment and now she pushes off, hard, the soles of her feet fierce against the floor of the pool. She raises her arms above her head and presses the palms together and suddenly, whoosh, here she comes, clean, high, centred, as if the water has been held down to allow this straight, glistening body to be released. He wants to clap, to cry out 'Great! Cool!' for the strength, the grace, the faultless execution of it, the languorous velocity.

She pulls wet strands of hair from her face and runs her hands over her head. She smooths the frill of her costume down against her thighs, straightening up and taking deep breaths, preparing to go down again. She spreads her arms out on the water and he sees her raised breasts as she fills her lungs with air. She tips her head back and sees him, and for a moment is aware of him, and then she is gone again, down ... down. He strains forward to see her, strains out over the water, against his arousal, gazing down into the swirl her body has left, and through which it will re-emerge.

And this is why he does not see it. Hears it, yes, somewhere in the back of his head, a sort of gurgle. But does not see the body, floating, face down, on the surface of the water.

The girl in the green frilly swimsuit is getting out of the pool.

Rossetti's Girl

The letter lay between them on the breakfast table.

'Typical Alice,' Adrian said.

'There's not much we can do about it. She arrives Friday morning, five past five Heathrow. Qantas. QF0319,' Meriel said, reading her daughter's sprawling hand.

'We're not expected to meet her?'

'Oh no. She'll find her own way here, apparently.'

'You never know what Alice is going to spring on us. Who is this girl, anyway?'

'Someone Alice met on the GAP trail, A New Zealander, from Christchurch. Is that the North or South Island?'

'I neither know nor care. How long is she staying?'

'Not more than a few weeks. She plans to get some work and an Inter-Rail card and spend the summer seeing Europe.'

'I hope she's got something to go back to.'

'Yes. University, at the beginning of October.'

'Thank God for that.'

'I'll get Alice's room ready for her. It may not be too bad, if she keeps busy and doesn't hang around. According to Alice, we're going to love her.'

'You may but I'm not, because I don't intend to have anything to do with her.'

Typical Adrian, Meriel thought and rose, sighing, from the table.

Meriel had estimated her arrival at around seven-thirty – an hour to get through customs, an hour, possibly more, for the underground journey from Heathrow to North Ealing and the walk from the station to their home. If she arrived by eight Meriel would have time to introduce her to the house, give her keys, and get herself to work by eight forty-five, in time to catch Assembly. So that when, by eight-fifteen, their visitor had not arrived, she telephoned the airline to see if there had been a delay. No delay, she was told, in fact the plane had arrived a few minutes ahead of schedule.

By eight forty-five she was both concerned and irritated. She would now certainly miss Assembly. She would have difficulty making her first lesson. Adrian had already left. She would have to leave the key with her next-door neighbour which she was loath to do, for a stranger. She saw no alternative. As she was hastily scribbling a note, the doorbell rang. She screwed up the note and rushed, relieved, to answer it.

'Hi. You must be Mrs. Gilchrist. I'm Jo, Alice's friend. But of course, you know that.'

Meriel was pressed for time, but she took in the tall, large-boned girl with full lips, dark, deep-set eyes and a quantity of thick, dark brown hair, centre-parted and held back loosely with combs. She wore regulation teenage travelling gear of blue jeans, dirty, well-worn trainers and a white T-shirt with *Your Planet Your Choice* across the breast. She stooped slightly under the weight of a large, metal-framed haversack, a rolled-up sleeping bag sticking out on either side.

'Are you all right? You've been a long time getting here.'

'Oh fine. I stopped to buy some fruit and veggies from a guy who was opening up his shop. They looked so good. I don't want to cause you any trouble, Mrs. Gilchrist, but I'd quite like to discuss my diet with you when you have a moment.'

'Yes, well, now is not a good time. I'm already late for work.'

'Oh, I'm sorry ...'

'It's all right. I will just make my first lesson if I hurry. But I don't have time to show you the house or neighbourhood or anything. I'll be home around four. Will you be all right here till then?'

'No problem. I'm all in anyway. I'll just crash.'

'I've put you in Alice's room. It's first on the right at the top of the stairs. Make yourself at home.'

'Thanks. See ya.'

'Yes.' Meriel grabbed her coat and bag and hurried out.

The house was quiet when she returned. Adrian was in his study and Jo, she assumed, was still asleep. She took a cup of tea to Adrian. He was sitting at his desk with his glasses on, a large pile of exam papers in front of him.

'Every year I say I'm not going to bring them home, and every year I do.'

'Well you don't have much time to mark them at college.'

'Other people manage.'

'They probably stay late.'

'Yes, but that may be less depressing than lugging them home. Look at this.' He pushed the paper he was marking towards her, a red slash through the last sentence. 'If only they could write.'

'First year?'

'Third.'

'What's the subject?'

'Feminism, broadly. Women painters hidden from history by a patriarchal conspiracy. Thank you Griselda Pollock.'

'I thought that was an interesting book?'

'It was. I just don't want it played back to me at half-speed and mis-spelt. I would like it if just a handful of my students could look a little further than the set texts. Show a little originality, a little flair. I could even forgive the bad English. It's discouraging, churning out students who are simply churning out what you've taught them.'

'There must be the odd one, surely?'

'Very rare. It's a depressing thought, Em, that students are, on the whole, irredeemably conservative.'

'Hi! Mrs. Gilchrist! Hi there! You home yet?' A large voice reached them from the top of the stairs.

'Who's that?'

'It's Jo. Alice's friend. She's been here all day. She must have just woken up.'

'Oh hell.' Adrian took his mug of tea in both hands and stared gloomily at the paper in front of him. Meriel closed the door quietly behind her and Jo bounded down the stairs, two at a time.

'Are you feeling rested?' Meriel pulled out a chair at the kitchen table for their visitor and raised a teapot above her cup, a question mark on her face.

'Is it decaf?'

'Sorry?'

'The tea. Is it decaf?'

'No.'

'I only drink decaf. Don't worry, I'll get my own tomorrow. I'll just have water now, thanks.' She got up from the table and quickly poured herself a glass of water at the sink.

'Is it safe to drink, from the tap?'

'Of course.'

'Good. Only some of the countries I've been in you have to use tablets. I was terribly ill in Thailand. I was staying with this family – they didn't know what to do with me. I think they thought I was going to die. I did too, for a while.'

70

'You didn't think of getting in touch with your parents?'

'Not much point. They'd only have worried. In any case, it's all a bit complicated. My parents are divorced. No, that's not true.' She paused. 'My parents are separated. I live with my Dad.'

'Your choice?'

The girl looked down into her water. With her little finger, she caught a drip running down the glass. Meriel put a hand on her arm.

'I'm sorry. Please don't think I'm prying. I just thought it would be nice to get to know you a bit.'

'It's cool. It wasn't a question of choice. I'm with my Dad because he's the one who's still in the house. It was my Mum who moved out. Just before I was due to come on my trip.'

'How awful for you. Do you have brothers or sisters?'

'Two brothers. Older. One at Uni. One working for a mining company in the North Island. They're both totally pissed off with the whole thing.'

'And you?'

'Oh, me. I try not to think about it too much. I suppose I hope that by the time I get home it'll have sorted out and they'll be back together. Knowing that it won't. Apparently now I'm older I should be able to handle it better than when I was … I dunno. When is this cut-off supposed to occur, between the not handling and the handling? Oh, I'll cope, I'm sure. I'm a pretty independent person. Now,' she got up and took her glass to the sink. 'What can I do to help. Just give me a job and I'll do it.'

'Perhaps you could peel the potatoes.'

'No worries. By the way, we were going to have a chat about my diet.'

'Yes?'

'I don't eat meat. I eat fish, and just about everything else. I'm not a vegan.'

Meriel managed a smile. 'And your reasoning?'

'Oh, world's resources and all that. Plus, barbarism of the way they're killed. But what I wanted to say was, I don't want you to go to any trouble. I'll just have vegetables when you're eating meat. Sometimes I might buy myself a veggie burger or something, if that's okay with you?'

'Perfectly.'

'Mrs Gilchrist…'

'Meriel.'

'Meriel. Thanks. I hope we're going to get along okay. It's kind of nice to have a mum again.' She ended her sentences with the interrogative inflexion common to her nationality and generation. Meriel smiled.

'She's a big girl.' Adrian was taking off his shirt in the bedroom.
'I didn't think you'd noticed. You didn't speak to her much.'
'Long fingers.'
'And feet. Her trainers are enormous. She put them in the washing machine and they've been banging around in there for hours.'
'Large features but a low forehead. Reminds me of someone. Can't think who.' Adrian took off his underpants and screwing them into a ball threw them overarm across the room to land on top of the laundry basket. 'Good shot,' he said.

It was about a week later, when they were discussing the job Jo had been offered behind the bar at the Coach and Horses that Adrian suddenly put down his knife and fork and said: 'Jane Burden.'
'What?'
'Jane Burden. Em, can't you see it?' He leaned over the table and taking Jo's face between his hands turned it towards Meriel, the chin tilted slightly upwards, the evening sun catching her strong features.
Meriel looked at her. 'Yes,' she said. 'Yes. I see it now. There is a likeness.'
'More than a likeness,' Adrian said. 'Oh, I'm sorry.' He released the girl's face and patted the top of her head as he drew away. 'Terribly rude of me. But it struck me so suddenly.'
'Please let me know when you're likely to do it again,' she said good naturedly. 'Was she someone important, this Jane Burden?'
'To a certain group of painters. You've heard of the pre-Raphaelites?'
'Heard of them, yes. I don't know much about them'
'She was the model for a number of them. And the inspiration. Caused a certain amount of havoc, actually.'
'I can't stand women like that.'
'Women like what?'
'Flirts.'
'I didn't say she was a flirt.'

72

'She probably was.'

'As you said, you don't know much about it. Look, are you working on Sunday?'

'No.'

'Good. I'll take you to the Tate. Then you can have a look at yourself.'

Meriel had looked up, startled, at the 'I'.

'D'you want to come, Em?'

'No, no. You two go off and amuse yourselves. You'll enjoy it with Adrian,' she said. 'He's a good teacher.'

'What did she think?' Adrian and Jo had set off quite early, seen the pre-Raphaelites, lunched in the cafeteria and then separated.

'Oh, not much. She found them sentimental and artificial, thus putting her finger neatly on the pre-Raphaelite paradox.'

'And Jane Burden?'

'She didn't get it. But look, I did these.' He handed her his sketchbook, looking over her shoulder as she turned the pages.

'They're all of her.'

'Yes. I wanted to catch her from different angles, when she was unaware. I followed her round.'

'Followed her?'

'Yes. What do you think?'

'They're very good. Wonderful, in fact.'

'She's wonderful. Look at the bone structure. I had to be sure that I could do it.'

'Do what?'

'Paint her. I'm going to paint her.'

'You haven't done a portrait for years.'

'I know. It's the face. How does it go ... *That face* ... something something ... *between the sun and moon a mystery?*'

'I don't recognise it,' she said. And thought: it's a long time since Adrian read any poetry.

The morning sessions suited them both well. Adrian's studio, north-facing, was at the top of the house. Jo had the late shift at the pub and although she often came in after closing hours, she usually managed to get out of bed and up to the studio by eight-thirty. Meriel had taken coffee in once or twice but Adrian had asked her not to, it disturbed his concentration and Jo's pose.

'What is her pose?'

'Standing. Leaning forward slightly, like Rossetti's Astarte Syriaca.'

'Nude?' Meriel asked the question as lightly as she could.

'No. Though I won't say it hasn't crossed my mind. I don't suppose she'd object. She's a pretty natural sort of girl.'

'So. Why not?'

'I'm not seeing her that way. I'm seeing her as an undercurrent. A lot of her is hidden.'

'A lot of most people is hidden.'

'Of course. That's why we paint.'

Meriel had not planned a busy summer. Two weeks in Cornwall at the end of August, as usual. Apart from this, she and a friend had booked on a poetry writing course and she expected Adrian to continue his funded research into English Land Art. She asked him when he planned to get down to it.

'Oh, I can't think about that at the moment. This portrait, Jo's portrait, it's taking all my energy.'

'It's going well?'

'I think so. I hope so. I must use her while I've got her. You know that she plans to go Inter-Railing in August. By the way, I've booked a table for the three of us at The Gate on Saturday night. It's a vegetarian restaurant.'

'I didn't know you knew about vegetarian restaurants.'

'I don't. Jo told me about it. It's in Hammersmith. Apparently it was Linda McCartney's favourite eating place.'

'Oh. Oh good.'

'What's the matter? You don't sound very keen.'

'No, that's fine. I was just wondering, why suddenly? Isn't Jo supposed to be working?'

'Hasn't she told you? It's her eighteenth birthday.'

Meriel asked Jo if that was what she wanted, to spend her eighteenth birthday with the two of them.

'It would be great. We're having a bit of a knees-up at the pub on Friday night but they've given me Saturday off. I thought it was so kind of Adrian to suggest it.'

Meriel started. She had not hear Jo call her husband anything other than Mr. Gilchrist.

'Well, we'd like to do for you whatever your parents would do.'

'I appreciate it. Thank you, Em.'

74

'Only my husband calls me Em. And very close friends.' Meriel surprised herself by the coldness in her tone.

'I'm sorry. It's Adrian. We talk all the time, you know. I didn't mean to offend you.'

'I know. I understand.'

Meriel discussed with Adrian a present for Jo. She'd thought about a book on Europe's capitals and he agreed. But he wasn't really listening. He had picked up a necklace from the dressing-table and was holding it round his neck, motioning for her to fasten the clasp. It was costume jewellery, not valuable, a large, garnet-coloured stone at the drop. He stood before the mirror, turning his head from side to side, watching the light bounce off the coloured glass.

'Are you going to wear it all day?'

'I could use it. The colours are good. And Em, you know that green silk dress. The one you used to wear to balls, in the days when we went to balls?' Adrian had painted Meriel in the dress when she was twenty. He had been entranced by her Celtic skin and light red hair against its darkness. 'Have you still got it?'

'I expect so. Somewhere.'

'Be a dear and root it out for Jo.'

'She'll never fit into it.'

'It doesn't matter. It's the effect I'm after.'

On Sunday Jo decided she would go to the Tate again. 'I thought I'd take another look at those pre-Raphaelite guys. Now that I'm somehow associated with them. You could come with me if you wanted, Adrian. You could give me your lecture again. I wasn't really listening the first time.'

'That's honest, anyway,' he said.

'Will you?'

'Of course. I'd be delighted.' He went upstairs and put on a dark blue shirt that Meriel hadn't seen since art school days, and a cravat. Tall, gaunt, with narrow features and greying hair, he had looked old even as a young man, but bohemian, interesting. He took his camera from a shelf in the kitchen.

Jo was waiting for him at the door. 'I'm getting quite into this art stuff. We could do another gallery next weekend. If you had the time.'

'Why not?' he said.

After they had gone, Meriel picked up a book, dislodged when Adrian had reached for his camera. It was a slim volume of the poetry of Dante Gabriel Rossetti. It fell open at a marker, where a passage had been lightly underscored:

> *That face, of Love's all-penetrative spell*
> *Amulet, talisman and oracle –*
> *Betwixt the sun and moon a mystery.'*

She shut the book and picked up the phone.

'Look, Tess, I'm really sorry and I know you're going to be mad with me, but I can't come on the poetry course.'

'What d'you mean, can't? What's wrong?'

'Nothing's wrong.'

'Something's wrong, or you wouldn't be telephoning. I'm coming over.'

'Please don't. I've told you, everything's fine. I just can't come, that's all.'

'We'll see about that.' Tessa put down the phone.

The two women sat at the kitchen table. 'I don't understand. It was you who wanted to go on the poetry course, not me. And now, with barely a week to go, you blithely tell me you're not coming. It's a bit of a let-down, Em, you must admit.'

'I know. And I'm sorry. I just feel I can't come away. Not at the moment.'

'Are you ill?'

'No.'

'What's going on?'

'Nothing's going on.'

'Where's Adrian? Researching his Land Art stuff?'

'No. He's gone to the Tate with Jo, our New Zealand lodger.'

'Lodger?'

'Yes. She's a friend of Alice's. She's staying for the summer. Adrian's painting her.'

Tessa raised her eyebrows. 'Is that it?'

'Is that what?'

'What's going on.'

'I told you, Tess, nothing's going on. Nothing. Nothing.'

Tessa had left by the time Adrian and Jo came back from their expedition. Their voices preceded them down the street. Meriel looked out of the window and saw two people, almost the same height, walking companionably together. Jo broke away to jump a hopscotch grid some children had chalked on the pavement. She stopped in the half-circle at the top and turned, waiting for Adrian to catch up with her. He put his arm round her shoulders and turned her towards the house.

She learnt from Adrian that Jo had saved up enough money for her Inter-Rail ticket. She planned to leave mid-August.

'I don't know why she has to go. I've told her, London has enough to keep most people happy for several summers.'

'I expect she's made up her mind. It's what she planned.'

'Yes, unfortunately. There's still so much to do. Young people are so inflexible.'

'Well, she'll be back, I suppose. Before she goes home at the end of September.'

'Yes, but only for a couple of days. She'll catch up with Alice, she says, then she's off. I don't know why she doesn't stay and do a degree here. Marine Biology. I'm sure there are courses that would take her.'

'Her home is New Zealand.'

'She could live here. We're flexible. I mean, Alice will be back and off again before you can say knife. God, the house will be dead without her.'

'Alice?'

'Jo.'

The summer passed and Alice came home and Jo returned to them, briefly, but her time was spent renewing old friendships at the pub, or chatting with Alice in her room. Once or twice Adrian brought up the subject of the portrait but Jo said she was sorry, but she really didn't have the time and didn't he have enough now to finish it? He had loads of sketches and what about all those photographs he took, on their second visit to the Tate? 'I mean, I don't know how painters work, Meriel,' she said, 'but if they're all as obsessive as Adrian I'm surprised anything ever gets finished. Have you seen the portrait?'

'No. He doesn't like me to look at work in progress.'

'Nor I. I asked for a peek before I left, but he said No. He's still got that green dress draped over a chair. I always felt uncomfortable in it. Oh, by the way, the Europe's Capitals book was brilliant.'

'I'm so glad.'

She wrote from New Zealand, to thank them and to ask for

Alice's e-mail address. The envelope was addressed to Meriel but the letter included them both. She hoped Adrian's research was progressing satisfactorily and she wondered how the portrait was coming along.

'How is it coming along? What shall I tell her?'

'Nothing.'

She raised her eyebrows.

'I've abandoned the Rossetti theme, you can tell her that.'

'Is that it?'

'I shan't finish it. It isn't any good. I wanted her in that green dress. I wanted ...' He met her gaze and looked quickly away.

'Adrian ...'

'Don't.' He turned and went out of the room.

She opened the kitchen door and walked out into the garden. The September day was already losing its warmth.

It had been nothing. And it wasn't over.

Short Straws

Amanda has never been able to understand the attraction of the Caribbean. She is glad she is not expected to go. Nevertheless on a cold January morning she rises before dawn to drive to her parents' home and take them to the airport.

'You were late,' her father says, after she has helped check in their luggage and settled them at a table for breakfast.

'Only a few minutes. We had plenty of time.'

'We were anxious. Your mother and I were anxious. We should be spared anxiety at our age.'

'Oh come on, Dad. You're not that old. Mum's a bit doddery' – bending to retrieve a spoon her mother has let fall to the floor – 'but you're okay. Only joking, Mum,' she says, replacing the spoon on the table.

Her mother raises her coffee cup carefully to her lips. When she sets it down she notices that a little pool of coffee has collected in the saucer. Her daughter notices it too. A shadow passes across her eyes.

'Excitement,' her mother says, smiling.

In the plane, sandwiched between Esme and an overweight Antiguan, Norman regrets, not for the first time, the economy class accommodation. Really, at their age, they should be able to travel in more comfort. But the difference in price ... he knows he will never feel it can be justified. Supposing one of them should need private nursing care? They were quite fit now, but in the future ... Esme never complained, of course. He looks at her, nodding over the book she is reading. Or is she sleeping? Or just nodding – a sort of concurrence with the book's author? She has always read like that. Hasn't she? He puts out a hand and covers one of hers.

'All right, darling?'

'Fine.'

'Sleepy?'

'Not particularly. I must say, I'm looking forward to some sun.'

'Yes.' Norman takes High Life out of the seat pocket in front of him, and begins to think about their holiday.

The thing about the Caribbean, they agree, as they sit on the terrace enjoying their first rum punch, is that you get a taste for

79

it. Or perhaps not a taste for the Caribbean exactly, since they know nothing of the other islands that lie between the Gulf of Mexico and the coast of Venezuela, and precious little of this one, but a taste for warmth. For one week of guaranteed sunshine and perfect temperatures, trade winds taking the heat off the noon sun, stirring the stiff leaves of palm trees into a soft background clamour. This year will be their tenth at Frigate Bay. Same week, same hotel, and very often the same people.

'Norman. Esme. How nice to see you again. You're looking well, I must say.'

'Thank you. So are you. Very well.' At Frigate Bay, you are either looking well, or you are not here.

Their daughter frequently asks them what they find to do at the Frigate Bay Beach Resort, a small hotel with a central lodge and dining area, and twenty individual cabins on the beach, and indeed it is not a holiday for a young woman in her thirties. Before breakfast, they stroll along the beach. From breakfast until lunch they read their books, or day-old English newspapers, under their individual beach umbrellas. A light lunch in the dining room is followed by an afternoon doing more or less the same. Or they might take a dip in the sea. Or Norman might walk about with his new digital camera. Norman takes a lot of photographs, particularly at sunset. Evening finds them in the bar in the colourful leisurewear purchased *exprès*, renewing friendships and drinking cocktails. Esme asks the barman, Henry, who has served in the bar all the years they have been coming here, if she might have a straw in her rum punch because with these long glasses and the ice ... the ice makes one's hand shake a bit, you know. Henry has noticed. He has put a tumbler of coloured straws on the bar. And behind the bar he has some shorter straws. He has cut them down and keeps them in a glass. So that when Esme orders a Martini or a Margarita, Henry has popped one in before she can even ask.

'Sweet, isn't he, Henry.'

Esme has made a friend. A new friend, Pamela, married to George. It is their first visit to Frigate Bay. She takes a taxi tour with her new friend. The driver, secured for them by Henry, is a man with many relatives since each of the tourist attractions they visit – a craft shop, a lacemaking factory, a pottery – appears to be run by a cousin. To whom they are introduced with much warmth and humour and assurances that nowhere on the island will they find better value, or higher quality work-manship. Esme's friend is in buying mood, which makes their driver happy. Esme resists until the pottery, and then, well, that glaze is prettier than anything she has seen in England and she has been looking for a vase, hasn't she. Ever since the Waterford crystal broke. Only a little thing. Easy to pack. Norman will not mind. She picks up a vase – not large, a deep, cobalt blue – and turns it in the light. Beautiful.

'Pamela ...' but as she turns to consult her friend the vase unaccountably leaves her grasp and shatters on the ground. Blue and terracotta shards glint in the sun.

'Did I drop it?' She looks at her hands, puzzled.

'It's the heat, dear. The glaze is shiny and your hands are probably sweaty. I know mine are. I wouldn't worry about it. You'll probably have to pay for it, though. That's the thing.'

In fact she pays for two, because according to the taxi driver's cousin, it was one of a pair, and breaking it has knocked the value off the other one. Esme fumbles in her purse for the money. She and her friend decide not to recount the incident to Norman. Such a terrible waste of money.

As their week nears its end, Esme and Norman invite their new friends, the Mathiesons, to join them for dinner the following evening. It will be their last night. Norman has walked up the beach to their cabin to invite them. He returns to Esme and they sit under the beach umbrella together, waiting for the sunset. Quite suddenly the sky darkens and before they can gather up their possessions and return to the shelter of their cabin they, their towels, their books and newspapers are soaked, the rain falling in great drops, heavy as hail. When, later, they walk up to the lodge for cocktails, they proceed under their rain um-brellas, their tropical clothing garish in the greenish light.

'This is a bit of a turnup, Henry,' Norman says, as they settle themselves on bar stools, the terrace tables and chairs too wet to use. 'What have you done with the sun?'

'She come back soon, Mr. Turner. Caribbean rain, it come sudden and it leave sudden. You don't need to worry, Sir. Rain is gone away quick quick, Sir.'

But Henry is wrong. The night throws up a violent storm, wind whipping white foam off the sea, rain clattering on to the corrugated roof of their cabin. By morning, the storm has abated but the sky is overcast. Esme walks out on to the beach. Chairs and loungers are strewn about like matchstick furniture, over-turned. Fronds of bougainvillea hang loosely from verandahs. From several cabins roofing has been torn away and lies, buckled, on the wet sand. Yellow and black bananaquits dart from pool to pool in the metal, sipping up the water with their humming-bird bills. The tideline is nearer than Esme has ever seen it.

Norman has joined Esme by the water's edge. She turns to walk back across the wet sand and he takes her arm. They watch as some of the boys wipe down and re-instate the beach furni-ture. Others drag pieces of corrugated iron up the beach towards the cabins. Further away, hammering can be heard.

'A lot of damage,' Norman says. 'Lucky we were all right.'

'Yes,' says Esme. 'We're all right.'

Esme chooses her most exotic outfit for their last dinner, a floaty two-piece in shades of green. Her slight frame and small features seem lost in its large floral print. Norman watches as she stands in front of the mirrror, struggling with the clasp of an abalone necklace.

'Here. Let me.' He takes it from her and opens the clasp, then slips it round her neck and fastens it. 'There. That looks nice against your tan. Did I buy it for you?'

'Yes. Last year.'

'It's pretty. I should have got you something this year. You haven't shown me anything you like this time.'

Esme smiles at him. 'It doesn't matter. There'll be other years.'

The Mathiesons are waiting for them in the bar. They have secured a terrace table overlooking the beach. The sea is still, the sky cloudy. The light is fading fast. There will be no spectacular sunset tonight.

George Mathieson jumps up, at the same time indicating to Henry, behind the bar, that their friends have arrived. He welcomes the Turners. 'The drinks are on me tonight. No, I insist. After all, it's your last night.' On cue, Henry arrives at their table with a large bucket, glasses, a white cloth and ...

'Champagne?' Norman asks.

'Why not? My treat. Thank you, Henry. I'll do the honours this evening.'

George pulls the cork and begins to pour.

'I say,' Norman says, 'nothing but the best.' Henry has brought traditional champagne glasses, not flutes. Esme, alarmed, looks at the four brimming bowls. Her husband and the Mathiesons lean forward to raise theirs. She hesitates, looking round. But Henry is back with his little glass of short straws. He pops one into her glass.

'You can't drink bubbly through a straw,' George protests.

'Oh yes, Sir. It's the Caribbean way. Mrs. Turner, she know these things. She been comin here a long time.'

Esme has leant forward and sipped a little through the straw, so that when George lifts his glass to propose the toast, she reaches out and, a little slower, cups her hand around the bowl and raises hers.

'Thank you, Henry.' Norman has lowered his voice. 'Kind of you.'

'No problem, Sir. Mrs. Turner, she a very nice lady, Sir. You take good care of her.'

'I do.' They took care of each other, didn't they. They always had. Life going by so evenly, and unremarked.

'To next year,' George beams. 'You will be back next year?'

'Try and stop us.'

Esme has removed her straw and is holding her glass up resolutely. It trembles only slightly.

'To next year,' she says.

Angel

She was someone you'd turn around to look at in the street. We could see this. Even when we were little, and not given to thinking much about things one way or another, we could see it.

Clothes looked nice on her and when I say nice I mean real nice, like they had been made just for her. She loved to wear things that sparkled, sparkly clips in her hair, sparkly motifs on her t-shirts. And everything pink. Her flip-flops, in summer – pink. Pink with a pink plastic flower between the toes, her cute little toes with the nails painted – you guessed it – pink. Her nails were so little it seemed a waste of time to paint them, but this she loved to do with the sparkly pink nail polish she bought with her pocket money from the five-and-dime. They were just eight little blobs, really, and two bigger ones which were the big toes, but my, how they sparkled when she stretched them out against our indifferent feet. Even though hers were black, and ours were white. And do you know, she did them perfect. Never had the polish run on the cuticles or if she did, she would wipe it off immediate with a Q-tip. Ma used to wonder was it natural for a little girl to take such care of her feet. She might worry about it, if she had the time. Mind you, she kind of encouraged it, because the two of us, she said, were a mess and let her down in a general way, so she was torn between wanting us, and not wanting us, to look like Angel. Or a bit more like Angel. Or just not like we did.

Christmas time you could have put Angel on the tree, she looked so pretty. Pa would pick her up and carry her up the steps and when they got to the top – which was the top of the steps and the top of the tree – he would put his hands under her arms and raise her high above his head and he would say: 'Shall I put my little angel on the top of the tree?' He would hold her there, above the tree and above his head, above the tinsel and the fairy lights, and she would do a sort of angel pose, or what she imagined was an angel pose, toes pointing down, hands above her head, touching. Actually it was a ballet pose, as I now recognise. Then he would bring her down and set her down on the floor.

'Put us up, Pa! Put us up!' we would cry.

'Not you two. You two is white trash. You two is a mess. I ain't havin' no white trash on my nice Jamaican Christmas tree.'

Pa told us that Christmas trees come from Jamaica and, for a long time, we believed him.

He also told us that in Jamaica angels is black, not white, and that was why it was suitable for Angel to be the angel at the top of the tree, and not us. Not that it mattered to Gemmie and me what colour angels were. No-one ever saw one, did they. No-one except Ma's Auntie Bridget in County Kildare and even she could not be quite sure. Anyway, Angel wasn't really black, not black like Pa. She was sort of black*ish*. Ma said she reckoned her ma, Angel's ma, the woman Pa had been with before he moved in with Ma, had been white. Or a bit white. Or maybe more than a bit. Or maybe she had some Asian in her. She said this, looking at Angel all the while. She said you had to wonder, when you got a child as beautiful as that. In our school Gemmie and me were certainly the whitest of the kids there, but Angel was not the blackest.

You might imagine we would be offended, Gemmie and me, being called white trash like that, but we were not. We knew it didn't mean nothing and was just Pa's way of kidding us along, like he did. Pa was as proud of us being white as he was of Angel being black. 'You two is little wonders, comin out white like that. Comin out like you'd been scrubbed head to toe with carbolic.' He would cup our heads with his big hands and hold our faces close to his and tell us to ask ourselves if we were not something special. He said it was down to Ma, her Irish ances-try. If he had known it, he might have used that word I've heard people use which describes people who belong to the Irish race. It's not a word that I'm familiar with, so I can forget it when I need it, which is now. In any case, Pa didn't know words like that. Pa was a janitor at some swank apartment block in the city. He wore a uniform and worked nights.

Sundays we got dressed up and he took us to the ball game. First, he would buy us popcorn and cola, then he would check that we were sitting comfortable and could see. When the game had started, he would point with his popcorn box at what was going on, and if there was something called a Home Run he would stand up and punch the air and ask if that was not the finest thing we'd ever seen. Pa was very content with where we lived, because it was so close to the ball park. Fenway might not be the smartest address in town, but to him it was just neat. Who would want to live in some fancy apartment block on Beacon Hill and need to come all the way down here every time the Red Sox played the Yankees, hey? Answer me that.

Ma, she loved the ball game also. She had her hero. And if this hero, who was a big blond player with a foreign-sounding name, if this hero failed to perform to her expectations, why she would stand and holler at him like he was her own son. I surely would not like to have been that player if Ma could have gotten herself within ten feet of him. We knew the kind of temper she had on her, us kids.

When she was ten, Angel told us she had become a woman. She said we should look at her body and we should look real close, because what was happening to her would be happening to us. Soon we would be growing up, like her.

'I'm not,' Gemmie said.

'Not what?'

'Not growing up,'

'Yes you are. So's Serena. In a year or two, I should say.'

'I'm bored,' Gemmie said. 'I want to go out in the street and play.' At eight and seven we were not yet greatly interested in growing up.

We didn't know that Pa had got himself a new woman, but Ma said he had. She told us when we hadn't seen him and Angel for a day or two. Jamaican men, they got a habit of moving on, Ma said. Most times they won't take the children with them, so she was kind of surprised that he had took Angel. Not devastated, you understand, just surprised. After all, Angel was not her child. We thought maybe Pa's new woman was so enchanted by her that she had asked to have her. Or maybe Pa just couldn't bear to leave his little girl behind. We were his little girls too, of course, but Ma would never have let us go.

We missed Pa terrible when he went. 'He's only just around the block,' Ma said. 'We can go see him if we want to.' But we didn't know which block, and Ma didn't seem to want to and it pretty soon became clear why. She had met this nice Irish cab driver, she said, who had given her a ride free, gratis and for nothing when she was coming home with the groceries. After that, he started coming round nights because, unlike Pa, he worked days. And after a time Ma said the Irish cab driver, whose name was Paul, had given her a baby and that he was going to live with us permanent and he was going to be our new Pa.

Gemmie and me, we didn't care for Paul too much. Furthermore, we could not bring ourselves to call him Pa. He had it out with us once or twice, but then Conor came along and of course as soon as Conor could say anything like a word he called Paul Pa, or Da, I think it was, and that must have made him feel better, and he let it go.

'Paul don't talk much, Ma.'

'He ain't the type. You'll get used to him.'

Worse than that, he did not take us to the ball game, and how Ma could tolerate staying home, with her hero batting away out there without her encouragement and advice, was something we could not understand. We supposed it was the baby.

At first Paul seemed quite delighted with the baby. He said he'd never imagined being old enough to be a father. He would peer at his son in his carrycot and make faces and funny noises and tell him his eyes were Ballymena Blue, and one day he would take him to Donegal and show him to the folks back home.

Ma said she was looking forward to us girls growing up and getting to be of child-minding age. So, I should say, was Paul. He would say, 'grow up,' or 'be your age,' when Gemmie and me fooled around. Which instructions kind of cancelled each other out, we thought. But we didn't say nothing. Although he has a pleasant smile when he feels like it, his eyes are not quite nice. They are small eyes, watery-blue. They are not that Ballymena Blue, which I take be the proper Irish blue, that Conor has. Paul is sort of skinny and young-looking – young-looking for Ma, anyway – but he isn't jokey or funny like our Pa used to be. Sometimes when he comes in at night he doesn't walk quite steady and then he will shout at Ma and say he wants those kids in bed. Right now. Doesn't a man deserve a bit of peace and quiet after the sort of day he's had? Some of the fares he's picked up today – Jesus.

Some time after Pa left, Angel started coming round our place again. Not Pa, just Angel. It was the new baby, she was just enchanted with him. She had never seen a baby so white, with such blue eyes. She called him her brand-new baby brother, which, of course, he was not. Sometimes it was as if she had never left. Ma said it was weird, but weird-good, not weird-bad.

Angel was growing up, Ma said, and making a way better job of it than we were. Conor had really took to her. We wished we were like her. We wanted to be her. Beautiful, nearly grown-up Angel.

After the baby, when she had built up her strength, Ma went back to work. It was a cleaning and ironing job, two hours a day three days a week, and she did it in the evenings, six to eight, when the owner lady, who was some kind of a lawyer, was home. It would have suited Ma to do the cleaning in her own time, but the lawyer lady was nervous about giving out the key. She'd been robbed more than once, and what if Ma was to be mugged outside the apartment, and the keys in her bag and all? So Ma went round her place, and if the lady wasn't back, she would wait outside until she was, and then she did her cleaning and had a coffee and a chat, and then she came home. She was a real nice lady, Ma said. Sometimes Ma might come back a bit late and Paul would be home and waiting for his dinner. Most times he wouldn't mind because Angel was there and helping with the baby or bathing the baby or showing Paul how to bath the baby – in which he was not greatly interested, I have to admit. But if Angel had gone back home and it was just us, then he would be angry and ask Ma what the fuck time she called this. Once he was cross because Ma came back early, which we thought was weird. He should have been pleased. We told Angel he was like that, moody, and that she had best run home.

Summer time it's real hot in our apartment, hot like you are all the time sweating. We have no air-conditioning, it's the same night and day, so we are always pleased when Ma can take Paul's cab and drive us down to Stop and Shop, which is so cool you need additional clothing to shop in there. Funny, isn't it, to have to put on coats to go inside a store. But Ma says we have to, and furthermore we have to take them off when we come out. Otherwise we will get a chill and die and it's way too hot to be lying around in stuffy little coffins, is it not. If we are thinking of dying on her, we should do her a favour and leave it out till the fall.

In August, you cannot take off enough clothes to get cool. You might save yourself the effort, it makes no difference. Outside is no better, you cannot run about or play. We would sit on the steps, us neighbourhood kids, and suck ice popsicles which we replenished now and then from the drugstore. They were raspberry flavour. Or we might go inside and try lying in a cold tub. Gemmie was doing this on that particular afternoon. Ma had filled it for her before she went out to do her cleaning.

I had finished my popsicle and got up to look for Angel. She would be indoors with Conor. I climbed the steps to our apartment, kicking aside the sticks, the wrappers, the butts of Paul's cigarettes. I thought about Ma coming home, and that we would get in trouble if we had not cleaned up before she did.

I didn't see them at first. The room is almost dark in summer, drapes pulled across against the afternoon sun. Conor was sitting beside them. Sitting on the floor, beside them.

I froze into the door frame. Then I went and picked Conor up and ran with him out of the room. He was bawling now, though he wasn't before, and I ran with him into the bathroom and Gemmie looked up and said why is everyone crying all of a sudden. I said I wasn't crying and she said yes, you are and I screamed at her that I was not.

Ma was tired when she came in. She threw down her bag and kicked off her shoes. She asked where Angel was.

'She went home, Ma.'

Ma said good girl, and went to the refrigerator, and asked Paul what he wanted for his tea.

We still sit out on the steps in summer, and the leaves blow about on the sidewalk in the fall. For a long time Gemmie missed her. Why had she stopped coming round our place? Where had she got to? She wished she knew.

Ma said it was probably down to us, Gemmie and me, all the time after her, all the time pestering her to come out and play. A girl growing up, she needs her space. Ain't that right, Paul?

Paul, he says nothing, and goes on eating his tea.

Old Tom

He was always there, sitting against the wall near the cash dispenser. We passed him every day, usually around half-four when school finished and the market was beginning to pack up. He wore a greasy woolly hat and frayed mittens and a heavy military-style greatcoat, in all weathers. His fingers were yellow, the nails split and jagged, but his eyes were very clear and restless, pale blue.

'Hey, boy! Throw me banana!' That was the first time he spoke to us and Jake had been quite frightened, the harshness of the command and the wondering which banana he was supposed to pinch, and how.

'From ground, stupid.' He had a strange voice. 'Ground' came out as 'grahnd' yet he didn't sound like a cockney. Foreign, probably. The stallholder reached down and picked up a bunch of bananas, past their best. He lobbed them to the old man.

'Thanks, mate. Next time you know, hey?' he said to us. His tone carried authority and menace.

It was the pattern of all our future conversations, if such describes what passed between us. For it was all on his terms. He never asked us anything about ourselves, although he was not unaware of our lives. 'You work hard in school, hey! Otherwise you end up like me, on street.' We asked him why he lived like he did, on the street. There were places people like him could go, we said, hostels. Jake's mother knew the address of one.

'You crazy? I proud. I very proud man. I free man also. I don't like live in house. I don't like charity.'

'Why don't you go to work?'

'Too old. Too sick. Wounded in war.' He rolled up a trouser leg to reveal – what? We couldn't be quite sure, the leg was so dirty and the exhibition so swiftly over.

'Who were you fighting for?'

'For you.'

'Us?'

'Yes, for you, you stupid. Polish navy. I join up at eighteen. No, I join up at seventeen. I tell a lie, how old I am. I grow up in Gdansk. Big Polish naval port. Beautiful city. One day, you grown up, you go there. You say hello from me, Tomasz, Tom.'

'Wouldn't you like to go back?'

'No. Yes. Maybe. When my ship comes in.'

90

He talked to us a lot about ships, the battles he'd seen, the boats his father, a shipbuilder, used to make in Gdansk. When he came to England, after the war, he had joined the Merchant Navy and travelled the world. There was no country he couldn't talk about. 'I free spirit. I citizen of the world.'

'How can you bear to sit here, day after day?'

'Okay. So now I citizen of Hammersmith.'

He said there were a lot of Polish people in London. There was a Polish café in South Kensington. He used to go there. Polish apple cake like you've never tasted. He didn't go now, he didn't even know if it was still there. He was ashamed, to be seen like this.

'You two, you don't count. You just boys.'

He never told us how he came to be 'like this.' He never told us any more than he wanted to. He wasn't grateful that we stopped to talk to him, or for small kindnesses. Jake had taken him some of his mother's apple pie one day.

'Is okay. Is not Polish apple cake.'

He dismissed us when he'd had enough of us, and if he wanted anything, he shouted for it. 'You gonna drink all that Coke yourself? Or you gonna share it with somebody needs it?' We worried about him when it rained, but he sheltered in doorways, wrapped in his old maroon sleeping bag. He didn't seem to beg – not for money. Jake thought he might like a dog, to keep him company.

'What for I want a dog? I got enough troubles, feeding one person.'

The market people kept an eye out for him. They made him cups of tea, and at the end of the day they tossed him their unsaleable produce. He said summer was a bad time, the fruit went off so quickly. Damages your insides, eating over-ripe peaches.

Last day of term, and we have money in our pockets. We stop by old Tom to get it out. We intend to treat him. What happens next we don't know, except that we are on the ground and the money is gone and there's a flash of steel and one leather jacket is telling the other to get the mobiles. And suddenly old Tom is up, and he has the two pinned against the wall by their necks. He shouts at us: 'Get up! Run! Godsake run! Go!'

First day of the holidays and we are heading back to school, or at least in the direction of it. We want to check on Tom, we want to thank him. Jake's mother has found a recipe for Polish apple cake. It looks a bit heavy to her, but she supposes it's the kind of thing he likes. She wouldn't know, it's the first time she's made it.

Jake is taking it out of the bag as we turn into the street. But Tom is not there. His patch is vacant. No familiar sleeping bag, no half-empty cans, no yellow fingers curling around yesterday's newspaper.

We run up and down the street, in and out of doorways, between the market stalls, calling his name. 'Tom!' 'Tom!' 'Tomasz!' 'Tom!'

The stallholders haven't seen him, not since yesterday.

'When, yesterday?'

'When we was clearing away the stalls. Round about teatime. There was a commotion. Some kids and two bigger lads.'

'It was us. What happened afterwards? Did you see?'

'Nah. We was clearing up the stalls. We didn't see nothing.'

'Was he all right? Did the police come?'

'Nah. Police never come down, did they Charlie?'

'Nah.'

'But you must have seen him since. You must have.'

'Sorry, mate.'

'But ... he was our friend.'

'Yeah? Well. Maybe his ship came in.'

Jack's Squaw

When do you realise that anticipation is all? That it's not the arrival, nor even the journey. Can anyone tell you? Could anyone have told me, four years old and desperate for the attention of my older brother?

He was going to be an Indian Chief, was Jack. He was going to be an Indian Chief for no better reason than he had seen the head-dress in a shop window in town and Jimmy Rumbelow had seen it at the same time and both of them had said: 'Bags I,' but the shop wasn't open, it being early closing, so it was a matter of who got there first in the morning. The party was in the afternoon.

'She's not coming,' Jack had said, when the invitation arrived.

'Yes, darling,' our grandmother said, 'you're both invited.'

'That's stupid. It's a boy's party.'

'It's William's birthday, of course. But you're both invited. William's mummy rang specially to tell me.'

William's mother and our mother had known each other all their lives. We saw the family often when our parents brought us to the small seaside town where our grandparents lived, and where our mother had grown up. William and Jack were special friends.

'It's still stupid,' Jack said.

'Well you're both going,' Grandma said. 'So that's that.'

'I still think it's stupid,' Jack said. 'Anyway, she's not dressing up.'

'Of course she's dressing up. It's a fancy dress party.'

Grandma spent some time rummaging around in her cupboards and discussing with Grandpa what I could go as.

'I threw away a lot of the things in the dressing-up box,' she said. 'It's a pity.'

'Why doesn't she go as a squaw?' Grandpa said. 'That shouldn't be too difficult. A band round her head, some sort of grass skirt …' he tailed off. 'I don't know. I don't know what squaws wear. I know,' he said, after a pause, 'she could go as Jack's squaw.'

'No,' Jack said, 'no.' And he stamped his foot.

'Well just wait a minute,' Grandma said. She put on her far-away, let's-think-about-this look. 'It might be rather impressive. I mean, supposing someone else is going as an Indian Chief ...'

'Which they're not,' Jack said.

'Well,' said Grandma, 'you never know. And just supposing they were, I bet none of them would have a squaw.'

Jack didn't say anything.

'I mean it would look rather good, don't you think. Your squaw would walk behind you, and if you asked her to do anything she would bow and say: Your wish is my command, O master.' Our grandmother's notion of other cultures was rather muddled. She lived a life of books.

'She wouldn't be able to remember it,' Jack said. But he was warming to the idea.

'No, all right, she doesn't have to say all that. She can just walk behind you and be your sort of slave.'

'All right,' Jack said. It was the word slave that swung it. 'But she's not to run off.'

'She won't. Will you, Ellie?'

She didn't have to ask.

I loved my grandma because of the adventures. I don't mean real adventures, because our grandparents never seemed to go anywhere. It was the adventures we went on in our heads.

She loved being things. 'Let's be Pooh and Piglet,' she would say. 'We'll go and look for heffalumps.' We would go out into the garden and start walking round the pear tree. Round and round. 'Keep your eyes skinned, Ellie,' she would say.

'What are we looking for, Grandma?'

'Footprints,' she said.

Sometimes we thought we saw them. But we never saw a heffalump.

We might be the Famous Five, although we were only two – three if Jack would play. Four with Grandpa. Or go upstairs and sit in a wardrobe. We pushed aside the clothes and closed our eyes and very soon we found ourselves in a distant country, a snowy country, where there lived someone called Mr. Tumnus, and a lion, and a White Witch. I didn't much like the sound of the White Witch and neither did Grandma. We tended not to stay too long in Narnia.

To be Jumblies she dyed our faces green and our hands blue with food colouring. 'At last I've found a use for the stuff,' Grandma said, and went on... *They went to sea in a Sieve, they did,*

In a Sieve they went to sea: In spite of all their friends could say, On a winter's morn, on a stormy day, In a Sieve they went to sea! She brought down a blue sheet and laid it out on the living room floor. The sieve was a large wicker chair that lived in our grandparents' bedroom. I realise now that it was a Lloyd Loom which might have retained its value, had it not gone to sea so much. 'And now,' she said, 'for *a beautiful pea-green veil, Tied with a riband by way of a sail, To a small tobacco-pipe mast.*' We searched through Grandma's scarves. None was quite pea-green. There was a flowery blouse in her wardrobe. 'That's sort of pea-green,' I said.

For a moment Grandma hesitated. 'Oh what the hell,' she said. 'I haven't worn it for twenty years.' She fetched a pair of scissors and cut a sail out of the back.

Grandpa wasn't a pipe smoker, so the mast was a wooden spoon. Grandma tied the sail to it and stuck it through a hole in the back of the chair.

It was a bit of a squash in our sieve, and the sea was nearly always choppy.

'Where are we going, Grandma?' I said, before I knew the rhyme.

'Deadman's Creek,' she whispered.

The Jumblies never went to Deadman's Creek, of course, but who wouldn't want a grandmother like mine?

Grandma said my hair was perfect for a squaw, black and straight. She found a wide red ribbon and tied it round my head, tight across my forehead, a knot at the back, and I looked at myself in the mirror. She said we'd have to do something about my skin. We went up to a bedroom, the bedroom my parents used when they stayed, and she picked up a tube of something. She put on her glasses to read the instructions and said: 'Damn. It takes too long to work.' So down we went to the kitchen, where she made a brown liquid with Nescafé. She made enough for Jack as well, because she'd have to do him later, when they came back from the shop. She dabbed it all over me with cotton wool and we waited for it to dry. Then we put on the skirt she had made me out of raffia.

'What are you supposed to look like, really?' Grandma said. 'I don't think Grandpa has much idea. We'll see if Robert Louis Stevenson can help us.' She went to the bookshelf and got down the old pink book she sometimes read to me. It had poems in it and lots of pictures. Lions and elephants, soldiers and circuses, fairies and chimney sweeps and little boys in top hats. She pored over it. 'Here we are: *Little Indian, Sioux or Crow, Little frosty Eskimo, Little Turk or Japanee, Don't you wish that you were me?* Good job your mother isn't here,' she said.

'The skirt's all wrong,' she said. It should be some sort of tabard. Silly me. Never mind, we'll make one. And with a feather in the back of your headband' – she kissed the top of my head – 'I think you'll do.'

We took off the grass skirt and she made me a little tunic from a pillowcase. She held it up against me and cut it short, just right. We laid it out on the kitchen table and I made swirly patterns on it with paint and coloured chalks. Grandma said it was beautiful. She said she wouldn't be surprised if we weren't going to have an artist in the family.

We heard their footsteps coming up the front path, and Grandpa's key in the lock. We hurried to the front door to greet them.

I stood there in my red headband and my tabard, feet apart – cold on the tiled floor – arms folded across my chest. Like in the picture.

Grandpa opened the door and Jack charged in. He pushed past me and headed for the kitchen. He was wearing a spotted red scarf round his head and a black eye patch.

Grandma looked at Grandpa. 'Jimmy Rumbelow got there first,' he said. 'Anyway Indians are really uncool, apparently.'

Jack's voice came from the kitchen.

'Can you find me a cutlass, Grandma?'

Strobe Lighting

'Who let you in?'

'Sorry?'

Music throbbed, strobe lighting pulsed green red red green green blue blue red, but here in the darkness all she can see is a shape.

'Miss Reader. My Miss Reader. Come here. Let's have a look at you.' He put an arm around her, drew her back towards the door. A bouncer opened it and they were out into the street, into the early, desperate hours of Ladbroke Grove.

He took her by the shoulders and looked into her face. He was taller than her, a lot taller, and had stooped to be at her level.

'Gorgeous,' he said. 'Still gorgeous.'

'Oh Robert....'

'Not you, me. Still gorgeous, don't you think? Still irresistibly gorgeous.' He stepped away from her and into the pool of a street light. He did a ta-da pose, arms flung wide, dark shirt straining against an incipient belly and sweat-stained from the heat of the club. He laughed and she laughed with him and they turned and walked down the passageway away from the club, motorway traffic passing overhead.

'Hey. What am I doing?' she said. 'I'm with someone.'

'And I've left a coat in there. What the hell.'

She'd always said that for a working relationship not to come unstuck you have not to mess around. You may not do that. It's off limits, no matter how late the hour, how many glasses of wine you might have had or how much fun. Or how rotten a day you might have had, and how much you would love to weep into your glass and have him put an arm around you and draw you to him and .... no. You don't do that. And because she didn't, and hadn't, yes, because of that they had been able to work together all that time and she had to say it had been the best time of her working life. Of her working life.

'Miss Reader will read it,' he would say, when a sub-editor charged into the office panicking about the possible implications of a piece of copy, an unattributed quote, an unguarded opinion. He loved saying it, never seemed to tire of it. To outside contributors he referred to her as 'Miss Katharine Reader. My

Right-Hand Man,' which was not particularly flattering but established the fact that he knew, had accepted the parameters.

'Why haven't you got it on with Kate? Or perhaps you have. Yeah, you probably bloody have, haven't you?' This, when she had been with the paper some months.

'Miss Reader does not fancy me and unfortunately for Miss Reader I do not fancy her.'

'Yeah, right. Like anybody believes that.'

But she was grateful for the steady denials, for the refusal to invent scenarios which would have been believed, true or not. The temptation must have been severe at times, with all the sex talk in the pub, after she had gone home to her Clapham flat and he had not gone home to his wife.

'You must be the only woman in the office, Kate, that Robert hasn't slept with.'

'Oh don't exaggerate. He's not that bad.'

'He is. You don't know the half of it.'

'I probably do, but I prefer not to think about it. Anyway, what happens to all these women he sleeps with? Supposedly.'

'It's not supposedly and what happens is they leave or get the push. Haven't you noticed. He doesn't like having them around after he's moved on.'

'Which kind of vindicates my position, does it not. You can't sleep with people you work with.'

'Can't? Don't say you wouldn't like to.'

'I didn't say.'

'You didn't say what?'

'I didn't say I wouldn't and I didn't say I would.'

'He really likes you.'

'I really like him. Really *like* him. It's why we can work together.'

'Got a boyfriend, Kate?'

'Uh huh.'

'Serious?'

'Can't tell.'

'Why not?'

'Too soon.'

'Bring him into the pub. Let us meet him. Give him the once-over.'

'Yes, maybe. Maybe sometime.'

'Miss Reader.' He comes into her office, puts his hands on her desk, palms down, elbows out and looks at her. 'Katharine. We need to have a talk.'

'Yes, okay. Serious?'

'Yeah, serious. Things have happened. Fill you in tonight.'

The Grapes is crowded when she gets there. He is sitting at a table on his own, a tumbler of whisky in front of him, his hand curled around the glass. From his flushed face, the slackness of his body, she figures it is not his first. He tries to rise smartly when he sees her, but it's too much for him and he slumps back into his chair.

'I'll get myself a drink,' she says. 'I won't get you one.' She's teasing but she means it and he doesn't respond.

When she comes back he is stuffing a wet handkerchief into his pocket. From the spilt drink? From tears? She looks at his face, his familiar, good-looking face. Crumpled now, the eyes that teased and twinkled at her red and watery.

'What is it Robert?' She draws a chair beside him, puts a hand on his arm. 'What is it?'

'Can't go home,' he says, or she thinks he says. It's difficult to hear, with the noise in the pub and his words running into each other.

'You can't ...?'

'Go home, I said. Can't .....' his voice is rising now and he's getting to his feet... 'she's fucking....' And then he falls over and lies on the floor and she takes off her jacket and puts it under his head and runs out into the street and calls a taxi and somehow he is got into it and she takes him home to her flat. There seems nothing else to do.

He lived there for three weeks, in her small Clapham flat, while he tried to sort his life out and cried about his children and phoned lawyers and estate agents. He'd taken sick leave but she went into the office, leaving him at the breakfast table smiling and waving a piece of toast, making an effort because of her, because of their friendship.

'Attagirl, Miss Reader. My reliable Miss Reader.' She'd always smiled at his expressions, quaint, old-fashioned, from some other era.

Some evenings she cooked, some evenings they went to the local bistro where he cheered up and drank too much.

'You do not know, Miss Reader, how hard it has been keeping my hands off you all these years.'

'Yes well, hard as it may be you'll have to keep on keeping them off.' They clinked glasses and smiled at each other.

At the weekends they walked across the Common and she listened. She listened to the mess he had made of his life, with the women and the drinking. No, he didn't want anyone else, he didn't want a divorce, he wanted his life back. It was almost as if she wasn't there.

When he came back to the office, she told him.

'Why, Katharine, why? I don't understand it. We're good together. We're a team. Is it money? It's money, isn't it? I'll get you a rise. I'll ...'

'It's not about money.'

'Oh for Christ's sake, Kate. What is it, then? Stay. Please stay. I'm begging you. Look ...' and he whipped off his jacket and knelt on it and put his hands together in a beseeching, prayer-like gesture and he looked so funny and ridiculous that she might have smiled.

'I can't, Robert.'

'Tell me why.'

'I just can't. That's all.'

He said it was worse than a divorce.

They wondered if they should go back, she to her friend, he for his overcoat. He could pick it up tomorrow.

'Playing fast and loose, Miss Reader?'

'No. It was a girl friend.'

He had clocked her fingers, taken in the ring. 'Married.'

She nodded.

'Happy?'

She looked at him. What sort of a question was that.

He took her hand in his and they walked on down the street.